The Places Between

by

Jacob Minasian

Finishing Line Press
Georgetown, Kentucky

The Places Between

ACKNOWLEDGMENTS

The chapter "Jackson and Marlene" was first published by Of Rust and Glass in the anthology *Dreams of Rust and Glass* as a short story under the title "The Places Between."

Publisher: Leah Huete de Maines
Editor: Christen Kincaid
Cover Art: Jacob Minasian
Author Photo: Helena Minasian
Cover Design: Elizabeth Maines McCleavy

Order online: www.finishinglinepress.com
also available on amazon.com

Author inquiries and mail orders:
Finishing Line Press
PO Box 1626
Georgetown, Kentucky 40324
USA

Contents

For my wife
and for my daughter

Part One

Jackson and Marlene

"We can't stay there for long," Jackson said, splintering more than two hours of silence.

Marlene stared at him from the passenger seat. "You say that every time, Jackie. Every time."

Jackson gave her a quick peripheral look. Not an angry look. Not a pleasant one.

"Jesus, you'd think I've been in a coma these past four years," Marlene said.

"Has it been four already?" Jackson's tone requested no response.

"Fuck you, Jackie. It just stresses me out is all." Marlene grabbed at the manual window handle, cranked the glass down halfway.

"Yeah," was Jackson's only reply. After a few minutes listening to the empty country air fill the car, "You think I like to be the one checking up on this shit all the time, Leenie? You think I wanted to leave Nevada? It was the best thing we had going since West Virginia. But someone has to listen. Someone has to be responsible. Speaking of which…" Jackson hit the knob on the radio.

Static was all that sounded.

"Nothing," Jackson said. "What I wouldn't give for a fucking iPod right now. A damn cassette tape would do."

"Let's just go back to the deafening silence," Marlene said. "At least until we find some damn aspirin."

"Sounds perfect," Jackson said, "next to a full tank of gas, air conditioning, and a cold beer."

Marlene snorted.

Jackson gave her a stilted glance. "Or maybe a drive back through California."

"Stop the car." Marlene didn't move.

"Leenie…"

"Pull the car over right now, Jackie. I mean it. *Right now.*"

Jackson slowed the '84 Mazda on the desert-fried highway, until the car and its attached storage trailer rested on the road's shoulder. Marlene snapped the door open and took a few quick steps away before stopping. She could already feel the asphalt's heat beneath the worn rubber of her Pumas. The sun had just passed its apex in the sky over the arid landscape, and she stared out at the sun-bleached brown of the dirt, the horizon's desolate undulations, empty save for a few dead tree trunks and branches, collapsed and weathered. She looked down and swiped at a tear she felt on her face before it had registered in her heart.

She hadn't heard Jackson open his car door when he stepped next to her, facing out toward the landscape.

"I'm sorry," he said. "Bad joke."

He looked at her, looked back to the horizon. They stood in silence for a little over a minute. She was grateful for that silence.

Jackson continued, "I just. I think I just thought we'd have more time in Nevada. The ocean, the beach. We haven't been to a place like that in a long time." His chin lowered. "It made me forget."

She was aware of how much he loved it there. The beach where they had camped had the faint resemblance to a tropical island, waves calm across the earth's grain. Jackson swam in those waves everyday. But she didn't. She couldn't. All she could think about was what had drowned in all that water.

"C'mon," Jackson said. "The ARWS last said that we should be well into Minnesota by sunrise tomorrow." He looked up toward the sun's position. "We have to go."

Marlene turned and guided herself slowly back to the car.

#

"Got it!" Jackson said from behind the counter of the abandoned Shell station. "I can't believe this place's backup generator is still good. Pump Three. Let's hope it works. Remember to fill all the empties."

"I know," Marlene said, indignant, a tone that could cut diamond.

She considered making a snarky comment about his experience as a Chevron clerk finally coming in handy, but passed on the idea. No time for that now. They should have still been on the highway, headed toward Minneapolis, but a standing gas station was too much fortune to pass by. The store's roof had been split open, the char marks indicating it was probably by lightning, but the tanks appeared to be intact, and the shelves looked as if they hadn't been completely ransacked. She picked up a can of three-cheese ravioli that had rolled under one of the broken refrigeration units.

"There's some good stuff here," she said, dropping the can into her backpack. "I can't believe we found this place."

Jackson stuffed a few rolls of toilet paper into his pack as he walked out of the bathroom. "You're telling me. But we have to be quick about... Oh, hey..." He appeared at the end of the aisle, an accordion of condoms unfolding from his upheld hand, bungeeing a few inches from the floor. "You sure we have to keep using these?"

"Yes," Marlene said. *Especially during all this*, she thought.

Jackson briefly looked wounded, and placed the condoms in one of his pack's zippered pockets. He disappeared from the aisle, but his voice carried through the store. "You should head out there now and get the gas going. I can finish the run-through of the store."

"Okay," Marlene said.

She began working her way back toward the entrance, but stopped at the end of one of the aisles. She reached her hand toward a shelf, withdrew it slightly, reached again and grabbed two boxes of pregnancy tests, shoving them into her backpack before exiting the store.

#

An hour after they left the gas station, the first signal of wind spoke itself into their minds. An hour after that, Jackson could feel it tugging at the unlit headlights.

They both bunkered in a knowing silence, the shared awareness that they may have run too far behind schedule.

"What does that sign say?" Jackson said, his voice heavy with the strain to dilute panic.

Marlene saw the highway sign, fallen from its metal post, leaning against the side of an overpass. All she could read was part of what she assumed was *Minneapolis*. The mileage was covered by either dirt or a large dark score from lightning; she couldn't discern which.

Rain began striking the windshield.

"I don't know. I don't know. All I saw was *Minneapolis*." She did not reciprocate Jackson's effort to hide panic. "Shit, Jackson, what are we going to do? Can you go any faster?"

Jackson looked down at the speedometer. "We're going one hundred miles per hour in a '84 Mazda pulling a trailer it's not meant to pull. Any faster and we could burn the engine out. Then we'd really be done."

"Are you sure?" She knew her question was superfluous.

"No. I'm not sure. Calculated risks, Leenie. Calculated risks."

They heard the first distant rumble of thunder. The rain became quicker and heavier, large drops drumming glass, roof, and hood. The sky was a darkening gray.

"Shit, it's rolling in quick!" Jackson said. "And we have no fucking idea how close we are!"

Marlene turned around in her seat, looking out the back window, her eyes large and her lips pulled back from her teeth. Lightning forked the ground behind them in shorter and shorter intervals, splicing the sky with light. The thunder became fantastical war-like booms that seemed to split open the atmosphere.

"Marlene, turn around and put your seat belt on!"

"It's getting closer!" she said.

"Turn around! It's better if you don't watch."

The car began to shake with each fracture of thunder. Jackson could feel the wheel pulling hard to the left in his hands. He wrestled to keep the tires straight.

"Oh, shit!" Marlene said, turned back, and grabbed frantically for her seatbelt.

In the rearview, Jackson saw the trailer lift off the ground. A moment later, the Mazda's back tires lifted from the highway. He braced himself, his hands turning white on the wheel.

With a loud metallic twang, the trailer tore from the car, and was gone.

The rear tires of the Mazda landed back on the highway with a wet squeal. Eyes mushroomed in size, every muscle visible in his jaw, Jackson once again struggled with the steering. The back tires slid, causing a fishtail that threatened worsening to a spin. The car slowed to sixty, fifty, forty miles per hour.

The tires gripped the road and the car's wagging surrendered to Jackson's control. He kicked into the gas pedal and the speedometer needle climbed clockwise.

The lightning struck the ground in front of them now, to their left and right, all around them.

"We lost the trailer!" Marlene said.

"Let's worry about that later," Jackson said. "We didn't lose us yet."

"That's everything we just lost!"

All their supplies, food, spare gas. Gone. And there was no guarantee they would be able to find any resources in Minneapolis. Just days earlier, Minneapolis was being ravaged by storms similar to the one chasing their Mazda now, similar to all the storms currently roaming the earth. The last calculation reported that over 78% of Earth was compromised by some type of natural disaster at all times. There was no telling which area would be next, which area would be clear, or what would be left after the storms had passed. The Automated Radio

Weather System was the only warning they had, the only way they knew which locations would be safe, and the routes to get to them. And now, with California and the majority of the east coast under water due to rising sea levels, there were less places to go.

"We didn't lose *us* yet," Jackson repeated, low, almost a whisper.

Just as he brought the Mazda across the 100 mph threshold, Marlene pointed ahead. "Look, Jackson!"

Jackson could see it too. Ahead, a break in the sky, the gray ending into a pure gold-lined blue. Just miles away.

"I see it. I see it, Leenie."

A bolt of lightning hammered the ground just a few yards to the right of the front fender. The shock rattled their skeletons.

"Shit, that was close!" Marlene said, shaking the daze from her head.

"We're almost there. Hang on, Leenie."

Lightning strikes continued to pummel the earth around them. The blue in the distance grew wider and brighter. The pedal under Jackson's foot touched the floor of the car.

The back tires lost their grip again. Jackson pressed the pedal hard into the floor.

"Hang on, Leenie!"

Marlene grabbed his hand as the tires lifted from the ground and gravity evaporated into weightlessness.

Bartley

Bartley's eyes blinked wide, bleary, then bit shut as a beam of sunlight caught his face through the restaurant's shutters.

"Shit," he said, wiping his forehead and twisting against the dark crimson upholstery of the dining booth. His stomach burned as his innards shifted. He squinted at the booth's tabletop, two bottles of Black Label Johnnie Walker, both fifths, both empty, one on its side. He had been too exuberant the previous evening after arriving at the 1950's-style diner in a small city just outside Minneapolis, finding the bottles in the bottom drawer of the restaurant manager's desk, one untouched, the other almost empty. Now his stomach swam with regret.

He snatched his pack of cigarettes, Marlboro Reds, that was lying beside the bottles, shook it and peered inside.

"Shit," he said again. Apparently, he had chain-smoked almost an entire pack of cigarettes too. Now, he had only two packs left. There was no predicting when he would find more. Regardless, he pulled one of the three remaining cigarettes out with his teeth, and reached for his Zippo on the table, knocking a salt shaker into its pepper counterpart.

He lit the cigarette—the metallic clink of the lighter's lid, the tiny crackles of tobacco and paper turning to cherry, the satisfying pang in his lungs. He tilted his head back and placed his left thumb and forefinger at the inner corners of his eyes. *Aspirin would be nice*, he thought.

He groaned out of the booth and walked toward the restaurant's register, located at the far end of the counter. The night before, he had focused his search mostly in the kitchen, where he found only rotted food and a random assortment of seasonings, and in the manager's office. He had not yet scavenged the area around the register.

As he approached, he let out a short laugh when he saw the register open and empty, pillaged by early survivors who still thought money was worth the burden. Bartley did a quick scan of the compartments under the register, and pulled open a built-in drawer just under the countertop. No aspirin, but four AA batteries rolled around the bottom of the drawer like drunken dancers.

He scooped the batteries up, felt the weight of them in his palm. His small transistor radio ran on AA batteries. He set the batteries down on the counter and carefully, from about an inch above the counter's surface, dropped each battery on its flat negative-plated end. Each battery stayed upright, signaling it still had its charge.

Bartley grinned, plucked the batteries back off the counter, scratched at his beard, and turned to head back to the booth where he had left his pack.

The hum of motors coming from outside made him stop.

He turned and walked slowly to a splintered window, peered through. Three men on motorcycles, about 70 yards out, headed straight at the restaurant.

Bartley jogged over to the booth and shouldered his pack. The belch of the engines was right outside the broken entrance now. He looked to the other side of the restaurant, eyeing a manhole-sized breach in the far wall. The back exit was blocked by a toppled freezer, but he could slip through that breach and work his way around to the rear of the restaurant, where he had parked his own motorcycle. He turned, his heart hammering, every muscle tensed to flee.

The motors died.

"Hey!" A voice sounded from behind Bartley. "Where you rushing off to, fella?"

Bartley's eyes were still trained on the hole in the restaurant's wall, the sunlight outside, the warming summer memory of it, which all felt miles and decades away.

"Turn around now." The tone was casual.

Bartley turned around. Two large men in jeans and leather biker cuts were standing just inside the entrance. They both wore sunglasses, but the man who had been talking, who stood slightly in front of the other, had his glasses up, resting on the bandana covering his forehead. His eyes moved from Bartley's face to the pack on his shoulder.

"Go ahead and put the pack down," the man said.

"No thanks," Bartley said. "I need to be moving along."

"Aw, come on. Stick around and chat. It's not everyday we meet a new friend."

The biker with sunglasses still covering his eyes smiled.

"Really," Bartley said. "Thanks for the invitation, but I was moving on anyways." He looked around the restaurant. "Not a lot here, but y'all enjoy the place." He turned back to his only exit route. He was not going to risk walking past the bikers.

"Put the pack down," the biker said again, this time in a shout.

Bartley started to smell something awful in the air. He turned back to the bikers. The first biker stepped closer. Bartley's eyes settled on the Beretta handgun the biker now held outstretched in his hand, aimed at Bartley's chest.

"Come on, fellas, I just…"

"Drop the fucking bag!"

Bartley's shoulders sank. He sighed. "Okay. You got it." He let the bag fall from his shoulder to the tiled floor of the restaurant. "Can I be on my way now?"

"How the fuck did you get here?" The biker's voice maintained its volume.

Bartley's stomach tightened. "My bike. Out back."

"Oh yeah? And is there gas in this bike?"

"Yeah."

The first biker turned to the second. "Check back there," he said, nodding his head toward the hallway leading to the manager's office.

"See if he's alone."

"I'm alone," Bartley said.

"We'll see."

The second biker disappeared down the hallway, and the first biker approached Bartley. The horrible stench grew stronger as his proximity closed. He now stood just a few feet away, his pale blue eyes feral above his stomach-length unkempt beard. Bartley stifled a gag.

The biker had a shoulder guard fashioned to his left shoulder, a dingy white plate, oddly shaped, with streaks of dark red the texture of rust. It took Bartley a moment to realize it was bone, broken from a human skull. The back of Bartley's knees began to vibrate. His eyes lowered to the biker's belt pouch, what looked to be a dried and stitched-together lung. And a band of human flesh wrapped the man's right bicep, a faded tattoo of an arrow-pierced heart, "MOM" spelled at the center.

Bartley's breath became deep and fast, laborious, as if his chest was compressed in a vice.

The biker tilted his head toward Bartley's pack. "What's in the bag?"

"Nothing." Bartley said.

"Nothing?"

"Just my stuff. Supplies."

The man's eyebrows lifted. "And a billy club."

Bartley looked down at the nightstick he had taken from a deserted police car. He kept it secured through a loop he had fashioned on the outside of his pack. "Yes," Bartley said. "It's yours."

"Mine?"

"Take it."

"Generous." The man smiled a yellow-stained breath. He knelt toward the pack.

Bartley's head oscillated like a lawn sprinkler, his eyes frantic, searching for a possible escape. Briefly, he wondered which item of the biker's outfit he might become.

Bartley's eyes anchored on a plastic jar labeled **Cinnamon**, resting on the counter just a few feet away. He took a slow step back, to the left, toward the counter. The jar was now within reach.

The biker lowered the pistol, reaching for Bartley's pack.

Bartley swiped the container of cinnamon from the counter, snapped off the lid, and flung the cinnamon into the biker's face. Half the container came out in a massive grainy cloud, making an audible smack of powder as it struck the biker in the face. The biker snapped his head back in surprise, his eyes clenched shut, cinnamon clumps forming around his mouth. He opened his mouth to cough at the exact moment Bartley hit him with the second half of the jar. The biker inhaled sharply, and barked in pain as a wild seizure of coughing overtook him. Brown paste poured and gurgled from his mouth. He raised the gun, eyes still squeezed. Bartley stepped aside. The gun fired. Bartley knelt and unsheathed the nightstick as the second shot struck the wall somewhere off in the far corner of the restaurant. He brought the nightstick down across the biker's forehead, sending him sprawling backward onto the floor. The biker lay spread-eagled on the tile, unconscious, blood flowing down past his ears, his breath spasming in sharp wheezes.

Bartley reached the mouth of the hallway just as the second biker, alerted by the commotion, emerged holding out a Smith & Wesson 10mm revolver. Bartley swung the nightstick into the biker's throat. The sound of the windpipe cracking was as chilling as the feel of it through the nightstick. The revolver clattered across the tile. The biker's hands cupped his throat. He jerked backwards into the hallway, a strangled intensity rattling from his body.

Bartley grabbed his pack on his way back across the restaurant to the breach in the wall. He lowered himself through it, feeling the memory of sunlight become his present reality, though he did not slow his pace to enjoy it as he trotted toward the back of the building. His bike, a single-cylinder, worn matte black Honda Rebel with a dark green trim, rotated into view, and an urgency and thrill inflated him as he closed the distance to it.

Bartley felt the sickening bright heat in his left leg before he heard the gunshot crack the air in the diner's back lot. He fell, his momentum carrying him down harder into the gravel. He felt skin tear away from his face and arms. Colors flashed through his consciousness. He rolled over, warm liquid on his skin, heat from the gravel at his back. He lifted his head, eyes searching.

The third biker was standing by the back exit, smoke bending from the barrel of his 9mm pistol. He lowered the weapon, and began casually walking toward Bartley.

"What'd you do to my boys in there?" he said. He was only about ten or fifteen paces away.

Bartley looked down at his leg, the wet red puncture in his thigh. The pain was nauseating. He looked back up at the biker. "They let me go."

The man chuckled. "Bullshit. Nice try though. I heard the shots. So what happened? They alive?"

"Could be. Why don't you head in and check on them?"

The man laughed again. "No, I'm good out here." He glanced at Bartley's motorcycle. "Once we knew you were inside, you didn't think I'd look for your transportation? What the hell is that anyway?"

"Good gas mileage," Bartley said. "And it's quieter than those Harley noisemakers you have out front."

"True," he smiled. "Lot of good that did you. Eh?" He was just four or five feet away from Bartley now. He bent toward him. "So how you get the drop on my boys? You ex-military? Ex-cop?"

"Chef," Bartley said. "I was a Michelin-Star chef."

"Michelin. The fuck is that? Like the tires?"

"No." Bartley spit blood onto the gravel. "Not like the tires."

This biker was bigger than the others, had a large orbed gut. He bent over it toward Bartley. "You know, you talk pretty cool. But I can smell your fear. Lost my sense of smell a long time ago, but with the help of my friends here..." From under his shirt, he unfolded a long string necklace of human noses, blood-crusted and graying. "I can smell your fear just fine."

Bartley turned on his side and vomited into the gravel.

The man laughed, a laugh that faded into a peculiar expression, his eyes studying Bartley's face, as if he had been overtaken by a sudden fascination. "Say, that's a pretty nice nose you got there." He holstered the pistol at his waist, reached to the other side, unsheathing a large bowie knife, dull and rusted with blood.

Bartley's head lolled to the left, away from the biker. He saw his pack, which had fallen from his shoulder, and lay double an arm's length away. He looked back to the biker. "Your boys are dead," he said.

"Oh yeah? Well if anyone knows, it's you. Get it? Knows?" The heavily bellied man crouched next to Bartley, the air so still Bartley could hear the jeans stretch to their capacity. The biker ran the flat side of the blade across Bartley's forehead, a sandy texture of dried blood, then brought it back across with the sharp edge, trailing an incision that rivered blood into Bartley's eyes.

"They're fucking dead, and you think I did that?" Bartley began to laugh. His vision was outside of his body. "I did that alone?" He blinked blood out of his eyes, turned his head toward the far intersection of lot and building.

The certainty in the biker's face wavered. He turned to look where Bartley was looking. Bartley grabbed the man's wrist and drove it upward toward his head. The blade caught the flesh under the chin, stabbed straight through his jaw, brain, the very tip shark-finning out from the top of his skull, steel showing bright red through the tangled mullet.

The man heaved. Blood fled his face onto Bartley's chest and right shoulder. The blade slipped, and Bartley drove it home again, hearing a crunch among squishes. He lifted his good leg, and placed his shoe on the bulbous man's collar bone.

"You've had a smell of a day," he said.

With a sharp kick, the biker, knife and all, careened backward into the gravel, and lay motionless.

Bartley rolled, stumbled, staggered to his feet. He slung his pack once again onto his shoulder. His dusted Reeboks dragged through the gravel. As he reached his bike, he fell to his knees, picked himself back up by the handlebars. In the bike's side mirror, he saw blood and skin.

Go, he thought. *Go.*

His bike pulled from the lot, the skyline of Minneapolis on the horizon's distant razor.

Logan

Logan Pierce twisted his fork in the lukewarm premium canned ravioli, bringing none of it to his mouth as he sat at the hand-carved oval mahogany table, in a room lit only by a small electric lantern and two thin white candles. One of the vegetarian ravioli split beneath the fork's prongs, spilling its cheese and spinach.

Logan looked up, to his right, staring at John's unmoving face, flickering in the low light.

"I know," Logan said. "I know, alright? But he shouldn't have started in on me. I told him. I told all three of you not to ever bring that bullshit up." He looked to his left, at Jonesy and the untouched plate in front of him. Jonesy, head sunken, face angled down, stared at the dark wood of the table. "Oh, you too, Jonesy? You fucking too?" Logan slammed the base of his palm down into the table, the porcelain dishes rattling across the luxurious grain. The ravioli grew colder. "I fucking told Marshall! I fucking told him! I told you all. Don't ever bring that shit up ever again. Right? And did he listen to me? No! So, eat your fucking food and shut up."

Logan stirred his ravioli voraciously, still didn't eat. He glanced up again at John, at Jonesy. His shoulders swelled with rage.

"I was a fucking *Senator. A United States Senator.* How dare he talk to me like that!"

Jonesy and John remained silent, staring forward.

Logan looked at Marshall, lying face down a few feet from the table, motionless.

Logan looked back to the others. "He was asking for it." He stood up from the table. "And he's not even hurt, okay? He's fine." He walked over to Marshall—a brown bag of rice with a face drawn on it, a T-shirt pulled over the fraying material—picked him up from the floor, and set him down in the seat at the opposite end of the table, facing the other two clothed bags of rice. "See? Perfectly fine. Now can we forget the whole thing?"

He sat back down. After a moment, "Look, yeah, I knew, okay? I knew, but I didn't know okay? There's a fucking difference." His heart dipped into his stomach as he felt his mind slipping down the rabbit hole of guilt. "I built this place for us. You three wouldn't be here if it wasn't for me. So maybe a little more appreciation, and a little bit less of this guilt trip bullshit." He took a bite of the ravioli, chewed, forced himself to swallow. After a few seconds, he shoved the plate away. "Yeah, I fucked up. I know, I fucked up. It's all my fault, okay? You all happy now? I fucking know it!" He looked at the faces around the table. "You know what? Fuck you guys!"

He snapped upright from the table and left the room, light swimming across the walls.

#

Logan Pierce stood at the bedroom mirror, staring into his own reflection. The soft sound of the generator through the wall, and the hushed buzz of electricity filling circuits and light bulbs, once unnoticed, were now inescapably perceptible, amplified by their consistent absence. Logan only turned on the underground bunker's power generator when it was absolutely necessary. Now, he watched himself with the lights on.

His face was much thinner than it had been when he had first moved into the bunker, his cheek bones more pronounced, even through the five-month beard that began an inch below his eyes and ended a few inches above his collar bones. His hair, once short and slicked back, now splashed past his shoulders.

Even through his wildly unkempt look, Logan was in love with his own face.

His eyes, slightly sunken, still sparkled an emerald green, and though his skin had paled, there were still remnants of its handsome glow. His eyebrows were thick and dark, and even in their overgrown state, were a pleasing contrast to his irises. He pressed a hand to his chin, ran it across the buried jawline that, paired with his devious yet perfectly symmetrical smile, had won him massive influence and many percentage points in the polls.

Now, though, as he looked back into the eyes of his reflection, and past them, through them, to the mind of the person hiding behind them, he grew intensely angry, a sickening fury in his gut. He wanted to let that fury out. His muscles burned with the urge to surge forward, swing fists into the dark waters staring back, driving knuckles into those glass eyes, with no regard for self-injury. But he could not bring himself to do so. If he broke the mirror, he would no longer be able to view himself.

A distant boom sounded from overhead, from the storm currently rampaging above ground, tearing into whatever was left of Columbus, Ohio. Logan looked up at the stone gray of the bunker's ceiling. He had seen this coming.

When he was a senator, he had read the reports, the ones published and the ones handed to him from his confidential sources, the ones whispered to him within the closed confines of a locked office. His colleagues in the senate had told him to ignore those reports, told him to shut his mouth and keep his hands open to the bribes passed to him from the fossil fuel industries, from the oil and gas and coal and car corporations. Just sit back and grow rich, they said. Besides, they told him, he would be long dead before Earth became unlivable. So he did nothing to stop it, even though he knew about it all. He kept voting to pass deregulation policies, and to block the eco-healing bills his opponents brought to the senate floor. He kept collecting the embarrassingly enormous bribes, and used the money to build the underground bunker in which he was now imprisoned. All while the climate grew more erratic, the natural disasters more frequent—earthquakes, fires, floods, hurricanes and sky-peeling storms. And then the disasters rose all at once, like beasts devouring the planet. And he had known it would happen.

His brain plunged into a wild spiral of thoughts. He looked down from the ceiling, saw sweat streaking his reflection, the skin on his face flushed red.

When these moments happened, he tried to tell himself that he couldn't have changed things if he had tried, that if he had stepped down, or spoke out about the impending crisis, he would have lost his voters, become an outcast, and another politician willing to cooperate would have stepped into his place. Sometimes this rationale worked to calm him, and other times his mind collapsed into crippling despair and self-loathing. He had known that the technology to save the planet existed, that they had fully electric cars available, and the ability to harvest clean power, but he embraced profit instead. And all those people—citizens, his constituents—died on his watch, while he quietly built his bunker.

His vision shifted askew. Nausea ballooned in his gut. He stumbled over to the steel door in the southwest corner of the bedroom, slid the metal plate from covering the keypad. He poked the green-lit numbers slowly, sweat dripping from his face onto his hand and arm. The keypad chimed and he heard a slight hiss of pressure. He grabbed the large levered handle and pulled it down, dragging open the door. The air felt different as he stepped into the gunroom. Cool and dry. It had cost considerably more, and wasn't completely necessary, but he had the builders make the gunroom airtight, so he wouldn't have to manage humidity levels within the room. It was the only part of the bunker the oxygen fans didn't reach.

The walls were decorated with mounted guns, matte black and camouflage, chromed and plated, glossy barrels gleaming in the automatic lights, everything from handguns to shotguns, high-powered fully-automatic rifles to bolt-action sniper rifles with over a mile of pinpoint accuracy, Uzi and Scorpion submachine guns, antique carbines, even one light machine gun that could fire over a hundred shots without reloading. He walked straight forward, past all of it, to the far side of the 20'x 20' room, and lifted a small handgun from the wall, black with a brown handle, a snub nose revolver "Saturday night special" that had supposedly once belonged to a famous gangster from the 1920's. Logan snapped out the cylinder, snapped it back in. All the chambers were full.

He folded into a heap on the floor, against the wall. Tears mixed with the sweat running into his beard. His mouth contorted in silent agony. He raised the revolver, and pressed the barrel into his right temple.

All the times Logan had done this, he was sure he would pull the trigger, as he was sure now, but seconds passed, and the determination and self-hatred ebbed into a deep and terrible grief. Everything became present, became close, as if sketched directly into his synapses. His breath, his mouth's parched texture, his eyelids squeezing more sorrow down the channels on his face. And he sobbed, and anguish finally heaved from his vocal cords. And he lowered the gun, and laid his face against the linoleum flooring.

#

With the generator turned off, in the dark lessened only by the lit wick of one candle, Logan was again slumped against the wall, this time in the kitchen, crying, his forehead pressed into his hands, rice scattered at his feet and around the dinner table.

Between cries, Logan continuously repeated, "He made me do it. I told him to stop. He made me do it."

The bag of rice named Marshall was flat on the floor next to Logan, deep gashes cut across the sack's fabric, a dinner knife still protruding from the drawn eye. Rice continued to trickle to the floor.

The other bags of rice, still sitting at the table, stared straight forward.

#

Logan stood, leaning against the wall, looking up past the rungs of the metal entrance ladder, his flashlight beam moving over the bunker's steel hatch, the only thing separating him from the weather outside. He had only been on the other side of that hatch once in the past four years, the only time that a clear zone had overlapped Columbus, only lasting a few days. Now, according to the radio, the nearest clear zone was in Minneapolis. Logan could feel the outside storm through the wall. He was beginning to forget what sunlight felt like.

With the world's human population whittled down to a small scattering, Logan had once hoped the earth would heal itself before he ran out of supplies. Now he was sure he didn't deserve such a future.

His skin was almost an ivory white in the ambient glow from the flashlight, large purple half-circles under his eyes. Gravity seemed doubled in his features, everything slack, sinking toward his feet. His eyes, and the beam of the flashlight, landed and stayed on the large wheeled handle of the hatch.

He had promised John and Jonesy that he would give Marshall a proper burial the next time the storms cleared.

Logan continued to stare at the hatch's handle, the beam shaking slightly as he imagined the other side.

#

The generator whined to a halt as Logan brought down the lever, the lights inside the generator room going dark. He left the room and entered the kitchen, two candles giving a sauntering light. He walked over to the candles and blew out the first. He took one last glance around the table, at John and Jonesy, each with a .38 round bullet hole in the forehead, and blew out the second candle.

Logan stepped into his bedroom, and lifted a comforter, sheets made of 1,800 thread-count Egyptian cotton, and a pillow from his bed. He walked toward the gunroom, the door of which had been left open, and looked down as he crossed the threshold, seeing that the outer keypad was dark, the inside keypad dark as well. As he closed the door behind him with a heavy metallic clack, a sharp panic gripped him, but quickly subsided.

Logan Pierce walked to the back right corner of the room, laid the sheets and blanket and pillow out neatly, and lowered himself into them. A warmth spread through the numbness in his chest as his head dropped into the pillow. And within minutes, he was asleep.

Nolan

The Atlantic Ocean off the coast of North Carolina undulated against the unencumbered sky, unmasked sunlight turning swells into jeweled dunes. The small stretch of beach below the hundred foot cliffs disappeared and reappeared to the water's rhythm, decorated with shells, green-brown bulbed lassos of seaweed, and driftwood smoothed by sea travel.

Nolan admired the hypnotic repetition of the waves within the pulsing landscape, brought the ceramic mug of morning coffee to his lips, sipped the black roast's bitter bite. Never cream, never sugar. He breathed his lungs full of saltwater air and turned to look up at the house, a white two-story with a red tile roof and thickly bricked chimney. Seagulls screeched overhead. His eyes found the upper balcony that ran the length of the back of the house. Soon, after she arrived home from the market, his wife Tori would be standing on that balcony, drinking her own cup of coffee—always cream, always sugar.

He smiled, pictured her there already, in her light magenta robe, fingering the heart-shaped locket around her neck, grinning down at him.

Though Nolan had loved his job teaching at the local university, whenever he looked at his wife, he couldn't possibly regret retiring the previous year, even at the age of 55. He adored his time with her, their quiet life by the sea, her painting in the detached cottage flooded with natural light, him working on his third novel in the upstairs office just off the balcony, adjacent their bedroom, a view overlooking her carefully tended garden and the sparkling Atlantic horizon. They traveled when they wanted, swam in the ocean in the long twilit evenings. He felt as if he was living in the epilogue of some epitomic romance, the place after the proverbial silhouetted ride against sunset.

A loud bone-vibrating crack shotgunned through Nolan's body, a harsh shudder that moved from his feet to the top of his head in an instant. He looked down at the grass beneath his sandals, found himself instead staring at the sky, his back slamming into the grass as the ground bucked hard beneath him. He tumbled, thrown back and forth over the back lawn, his head striking a sprinkler, an ornamental stone squirrel flashing through his vision. Dazed, he couldn't stand, so he rolled in the direction away from the cliff. He rolled, and mid-roll, he felt half the land at his back fall away. He twisted through one more rotation before he paused, looked back. Thirty yards of the land had collapsed. He was four feet from the edge of the newly shaped cliff. Seagulls careened into the cliff's sheer face, some clambering across the grass. A wild energy seized him, and he staggered to his feet, began to run. The ocean behind him tossed with ship-smashing fury. Tiny white triangles, small specks of sails, were swallowed by the frothing water. Nolan ran, warm blood on his forehead, a stabbing pain in his foot, one of his sandals missing. He was out at the road now, and ignored the gravel biting into his left foot as he continued to run.

He looked over his shoulder before following the final bend of the road, and saw the house, that perfect epilogue, disintegrating, slipping into the sea.

#

Nolan jolted upright in his sleeping bag, giving a short yell as he pulled himself from the nightmare. "Shit," he said, lifting the sleeping bag to see his clothes soaked through with sweat.

He looked up at his surroundings, the converging backlots of two hotels, a department store, and a restaurant, all off the exit that emptied a freeway into Minneapolis. He shuffled out of his sleeping bag, and pushed against the dumpster he had folded himself behind the night before. The morning was hot and unmoving, smelled terrible. He stepped away from the dumpster. Flies bothered the long-rotted garbage at the back of each building. Nolan walked across the backlot to the department store dumpster, behind which he had stashed his high-performance hiking backpack. He never slept with his pack. When stumbled upon, strangers took everything from a person.

He shouldered his pack, looked up at the glaring sky, shaped to an eye between the tops of the buildings. He squinted, looked down, tried to shake away the nightmare, its memory. The earthquake was only the third he had felt in his life, and it had stolen everything from him.

Nolan rolled his sleeping bag and tied it to his pack, walked down an alleyway toward the front of one of the hotels, a Hampton Inn.

As he emerged from the alley onto the sidewalk of the street, he heard the sound of a motor. He stopped for less than a second, pivoted and dropped behind the skeleton of a '94 Toyota Corolla, its hood gaping and its engine gone. The motor grew louder, and Nolan lifted his head, peered through the broken passenger and driver-side windows. He saw a man on a small black motorcycle crossing the intersection between the freeway and the mouth of the hotel's street.

About sixty yards away, the man on the bike had the appearance of a zombie, blood running from his mouth and forehead, the skin between his blood and his beard a pale gray. The rider's hand pressed hard against his red-soaked left pant leg, though there was no panic in his features. To Nolan, he appeared calm. The rider disappeared down an adjacent street, and the motor's thrum dwindled into silence.

Nolan closed his eyes, sank back down with his back against the Corolla. He breathed slowly, realized that his body was locked with tension from seeing a person in that desperate condition. He opened his eyes and looked up, his muscles slowly unknotting. Battered and deteriorating city buildings stared down at him. He looked down at the front of the hotel, where he had spray-painted his message for Tori, next to the collapsed entrance.

In bright red paint, he had written **Tori, I'm where I carry my love for you. Nolan.**

Tori used to joke that Nolan had a big backside, and Nolan would say that it was so big because it was where he carried his love for her. They both laughed every time. He was hoping that she would see the message, and check the backside of the building.

Nolan stood up with a deliberate slowness.

He hadn't seen his wife since she had left for the store on the day of the earthquake. If he thought about it long enough, he could feel it begin to break him, his shoulders losing structure, a mountainside that a single synapse could avalanche.

Nolan had desperately tried to find his wife among the chaos and the injured, massive crowds scrambling for survival. He knew she would be doing the same for him, could often picture her one street over from his location, moving in the opposite direction, always just out of sight.

Phone services had already died, and there was a conflicting surge between those trying to organize, and those looting and reveling in the anarchy.

Less than a day later, the first tsunami hit.

When the first ARWS message crackled over the radios, it had given instructions for clear zones, two that were reachable from North Carolina—Albany, New York and Grand Rapids, Michigan. Nolan had minutes to make his decision. He and Tori had been to Grand Rapids before, and loved it there, but they had always wanted to go to New York, and had talked frequently about making it their next trip. He had to make a guess at which city she would choose, and because it was closer, he chose Albany. Since making that decision, he had yet to see any sign of her.

For over four years, in each clear zone he went to, he tried to find landmarks from their history together—favorite restaurants, stores, places they may have visited over the course of their travels. He would find one of those places, and would wait for her until he had to leave for the next clear zone.

Now, he stood staring at his spray-painted message on the front of their favorite hotel chain. Wherever they had traveled, if there was a Hampton Inn, that's where they stayed.

He had been at this location for a day, but impatience boiled his insides.

Nolan looked left, toward the freeway, then up the street the opposite way, only seeing abandoned cars—eaten by time, lightning, fires, and riots—trash and shrapnel lying where the last storm had dropped them. He swung his pack around and rested it on the back end of the Corolla. He pulled a spray can from inside the pack and walked over to the front wall of the hotel. He shook the can three times, and sprayed over the words he had painted the day before, until they were completely covered, indistinguishable from the new paint.

He returned to his pack, seeing the label of the pinot noir bottle inside as he returned the paint can. The wine was not an exceedingly fancy bottle—about 30 or 40 dollars depending on which coast you were on—but it had been his and Tori's favorite. Nolan had been astounded when he stumbled across it. He received it as a good omen. And he saved the bottle for when he and Tori found each other in the new world.

#

A block into the city from the hotel, Nolan trotted to his car, which he had parked with the dented front end against the metal pole of a stoplight. When he had originally found the car, a dark blue 2008 Toyota Camry, it had been driven into a telephone pole, the keys still in the ignition. It had a considerable concave of damage on the front end, but not so much that it had damaged the engine, and Nolan had been surprised to find that the car ran perfectly. Even one of the headlights still worked. Wherever he parked now, he would gently roll the damaged front end to caress a pole or a rail or the corner of a building, to disguise it from the attention of pirates and scavengers.

Nolan took one last look back down the block toward the hotel. He had waited for Tori at three other Hampton Inn's over the years.

Maybe she didn't view them with as much significance. Maybe there were other places he was overlooking, or not looking deep enough for, other places to which she had more prominent memories attached. He needed to move on.

Nolan un-pocketed the keys and dropped himself into the Camry, slinging his backpack onto the passenger seat.

He had only driven a few blocks before he saw a white SUV, all doors open, stopped in the leftish center of an intersection. He took his foot off the gas pedal.

Four people—a man and a woman in their twenties, and an older man and woman in their fifties—were on their knees in the far left corner of the intersection, their hands held to their heads. Beside them, a large man in camouflage pants and a dark commando vest over a black undershirt held a large caliber clip-fed pistol. Nolan squinted. The gunman wore a Halloween mask—a melted face—and looked up from his captives as Nolan's vehicle closed in twenty yards from the intersection.

The captives, knees bleeding against asphalt, turned to the approaching vehicle, expressions desperate, panicked. Nolan's jaw went slack, his head rotating as he passed the SUV, his eyes bolted to the scene.

The gunman raised the pistol toward the Camry.

Nolan slammed his right foot back into the gas pedal as the first shot slammed into the back left passenger window, splashing glass through the interior. The car punched forward. Another shot struck the body of the car, another the front driver's glass—a trajectory Nolan assumed he barely escaped—but he was through the intersection now, bits of glass across his arms and shoulders. In his rearview, he saw the gunman step away from the captives, lining up his aim at the Camry. A bullet smashed the back windshield. Nolan ducked below the headrest, looked ahead, concentrated on the street, hands squeezing the wheel.

The gunfire stopped.

Nolan straightened, looked back to the rearview. The masked man had been tackled by the four captives, had been taken to the ground, struggling against their collective weight. One of the captives, the young man, rolled away with the gun in his hands. He rose to his feet over the scuffle—the other captives four-limbing out of the way—and fired a shot into the masked man's head.

Nolan cranked the wheel, turned left down a perpendicular street, the scene sliding from view.

He looked down at the fuel gauge in his car, reading a quarter tank. His adrenaline weighted his foot, the speedometer reading over 70 mph, the dilapidated district of brightly colored shops and restaurants blurring around him. Across the Mississippi River, a storm flashed in the gray-black clouds over St. Paul. He had three gas cans in the trunk, only one with fuel, and it was two-fifths full. He would have to find more in order to reach the next clear zone.

Every gas station Nolan had recently seen had been pulverized or rendered inoperable by the storms. Soon, he would have to resort to residential areas, as he had done times before, rummaging through garages for gas cans stored for household utilities like lawnmowers and leaf blowers. It was a process that consumed priceless time, and some of the cans were filled with the older kind of gas that rotted. After the worldwide gasoline shortage a few years before the storms hit, a new kind of gasoline had been invented, one that didn't expire and allowed cars to run longer, even raising some cars' efficiency by 130 miles per gallon. There were people, though, that had still hoarded remnants of the former gasoline, all of which had soured.

Nolan calmed himself to forty miles an hour, evaluated his environment. He was now in a poorer commercial district, streets lined with liquor stores and check-cashing businesses, used-car lots and fast-food chains. He glanced at a Long John Silver's as he drove by, snapped his head to the left, and kicked hard into the brake pedal, tires crying to a stop. He paused, looked disbelievingly at the center of the steering wheel, up to his rearview, and shifted the Camry into reverse. He backed the car up until it sat on the street in front of the Long John Silver's, and he exited the car.

Nolan looked up at the sign below the restaurant's logo, the sign with the rearrangeable letters, where they usually advertised the newest fried shrimp sandwich or cost-effective meal deal. Two letters and an ampersand were left on the sign: **T & N**.

His eyes dropped to the discarded pile of letters under the sign.

A Long John Silver's was where he first met her.

Nolan had been in the drive-through, fumbling through the greasy bags the cashier handed to him, making sure his order was all there, and Tori had honked at him from the car behind. He could still picture her face in his rearview, bent in frustration. Nolan was a graduate student at the time; Tori worked in an art gallery; they were both in their twenties.

Nolan had smiled, given a short wave, and paid for Tori's order at the window before pulling away. A few minutes later, she pulled next to him while he was eating in the parking lot.

Nolan hadn't thought of that moment in a long while, hadn't thought of Long John Silver's as a place he should wait for her, and now there was a sign in front of him that could be from her. She could be inside.

Nolan sprinted to the entrance, pulled the broken door as open as it would go, and sidled into the restaurant.

Inside, dust snow-globed the sunlight entering through jagged gaps torn in the roof, and through the large panes of glass along the walls of the building. Debris covered the floor and tables, dead wires drooping and swaying from the ceiling like artificial vines. Nolan looked around with size-whitened eyes, blinking hard, from the registers to the **Employee's Only** door, to the hallway with the bathrooms.

"Tori?" he said. Again, louder, "Tori?"

No response, no visible movement. Nolan stepped toward the registers, looked beyond, into the compact kitchen. Seeing nothing, his eyes cascaded to the register counter.

Between the two registers, neatly cradled in a pile of ceiling debris, was a gold heart-shaped locket, its chain wound around an apple-sized chunk of plaster.

Nolan gently picked up the locket, the plaster crumbling to the floor, and opened the heart. Inside was a picture of his son, their son, their only child, as an infant. Nolan's eyes burned. Tears shined his face. He now had the answer to the question he had refused to ask himself since the day of the earthquake. Tori wasn't dead, hadn't been dead this whole time. She was alive. And she was looking for him.

"Tori!" he shouted, bolting through the restaurant, through the kitchen, the offices, the hallway, checking each bathroom.

He slipped back out of the entrance and ran to the curb of the street, looking around in all directions. "Tori!" he shouted again, and kept shouting, his eyes frantically searching the street's storm-hammered landscape. Nobody yelled back. Nothing happened.

After ten minutes of shouting, Nolan walked back into the restaurant, sat with his back resting against the counter. He studied the locket, dangling from his fingers. He turned it over, seeing their son's name, Bryce, engraved on the back. He ran his thumb over the letters.

Nolan had given the locket to Tori for her 47th birthday, fifteen years after their son had died from a rare blood disease, fourteen years after the grief from the death had nearly ended their marriage. The locket was a reminder, an emblem of them staying together, of being able to find a kind of happiness again, being able to think and talk about and remember their son with joy, not just pain. He was proud of the place they had gotten back to.

Nolan looked at his son's picture.

He would stay until she came back, he decided. The clear zone wasn't supposed to last much longer, less than a week, but if she wasn't back by its end, he would stay.

He would wait for her.

Nora

The elderly man, about 70 years old, sat on the curb at the corner of the intersection, skinny arms turned inward, knees on elbows, frail hands dangling in front of a white beard that ran to the ground, its tip brushing the asphalt the same as the waist-length hair that stemmed from the sides and back of his scalp, which was otherwise bald and glistening, mottled with age spots, his scabbed and withered face twisted in heavy sobs. When Nora saw him, she knew she had to stop the SUV.

"What are you doing?" Chase said from the passenger seat.

"I'm stopping the car, Chase," Nora said. "Look at him. He needs help. I'm just going to ask if he's okay."

"We don't have time for this. And it's dangerous."

"Dangerous? Look at him."

"I am, Nora. I am looking at him."

The SUV rolled to a stop in the intersection, around 15 yards from the stranger.

"I'm with Chase," came a voice from the back seat, her mom's. "We can't be too careful. I don't like this."

Nora looked into the rearview at her parents, Debra and Winston, their faces tightened by concern.

"It'll be okay, Mom," she said. "I don't like it either, but we can't just keep going. I'm just going to ask him."

"I don't know, Nora," Winston said. "I mean, what do we even have to offer? A little food? Enough for one meal?"

Nora looked over her shoulder. "That may be enough."

"Doesn't look like it," Chase said.

Nora turned to her husband, put a hand on his, looked steadily into his eyes. "It'll be okay, Chase."

She turned and opened the door, raising her head above its top edge, one foot on the road, the other still in the car.

"Hey!" she shouted. "You okay?"

The man didn't look up.

Nora repeated "You okay?"

The elderly man seemed to get more upset, dropping his face into his hands, his shoulders heaving.

Nora glanced back into the SUV. Chase stared at her, shook his head.

She put up a finger: *one more try.*

"Hey," she said. Her right foot dropped out of the car, met the asphalt. She took one step out from the cover of the car door. "Buddy, you okay?"

"Nora!" Chase yelled.

"Don't move!" came a shout from behind Nora and to her left. At the corner directly across the crosswalk from the elderly man, a man in a mask stepped out from behind the wreckage of a black van, holding up a large chromed handgun. "Don't you fucking move."

Nora's hands instinctively went up. She heard Chase curse sharply in the SUV.

"Step away from the car, now!" the masked man shouted. "The rest of you, get the fuck out."

Nora heard all the SUV's doors open. She turned from the masked man back to the elderly man on the curb. He observed the scene, and when he saw her looking at him, he smiled a wry broken-toothed smile. He stood up, and with a quickness that was both surprising and eerily animalistic, ran to the corner entrance of the nearest building, and disappeared inside.

Nora turned back to the masked man, who wore military pants and a vest over a black sleeveless shirt, revealing heavily muscled arms. The mask had a long nose and blushed cheeks, and the skin appeared to be melting. She wasn't sure if the mask was designed that way, or if the man had melted it himself.

"All of you, around the car, now, over here," the man said, directing them toward the corner of the intersection where the elderly man had been sitting.

Her husband and parents joined her as she walked, all with their hands on their heads. Her parents looked at her. Chase didn't.

A few feet from the curb, the man stopped them. "Far enough. On your knees."

Now Chase looked at Nora, though not with the expression she anticipated. There was no blame, no anger.

The two couples settled to their knees.

"Now choose," the man said, standing in front of them. Behind the mask, his eyes moved from face to face.

Nora breathed hard. "Choose?"

"Who goes?" The man raised the pistol and turned it in the air.

"You don't have to do this. Take whatever you want. You don't have to kill any of us," Nora said.

The man's eyes flickered in the mask's eyeholes. "One goes now." His voice was a slow rattle. "Choose."

Nora's chest and shoulders kicked with each breath. She was wearing shorts, and the skin on her knees opened against the damaged road surface.

"Me," Chase said. "Me, we choose me."

"Chase!" Nora said.

"No, me! Us!" Debra said. She looked at Winston, who seemed to shake his shock.

"Yes, no, me! I'm in charge. It's me. Kill me," Winston said. "Kill me!"

Nora's mind was a wash of regret and prayer.

"So it's you?" The masked man raised the gun, leveled it at

Winston's forehead.

"No!" Chase said.

"Fuck you, no, it's me, Chase!" Winston yelled in a tone he had never used before.

"Chase!" Nora said.

"Winston," Debra said. "Winston, I love you."

"I love…" Winston started.

The entirety of the scene was sliced by the sound of an engine, a car engine, growing nearer. The masked man looked up toward the sound.

When Chase turned to look, Nora, Debra, and Winston turned also.

A car slowed into the intersection. The driver, a scruffy-faced man that looked to be in his fifties or sixties, stared out the window at them. Terror inflated his features as his eyes mapped the situation. In her periphery, Nora saw the masked man raise his pistol.

The car jumped forward with acceleration as bullets blistered the air, taking out some of the car's windows and thunking against its body. The car left the intersection, its speed climbing, and the masked man stepped away from his four captives to get a better angle.

Chase was the first one up, charging at the gunman, and Nora and the others followed. Chase grabbed at the gun as he rammed his shoulder into the left side of the man's body. The gunman staggered, struggling against the force of the hit and Chase's grip on the pistol. Debra dove into his legs at the same time Winston threw his weight behind Chase's. Nora leapt forward into the group of bodies, reaching around her father to drive her hand into the side of the man's head. They all went hard to the ground. The masked man grunted in pain as he took the full force of the fall with their weight on top of him. Chase wailed with exertion. Nora brought the bottom of her open palm down into the man's left ear repeatedly.

Chase rolled out of sight, came back standing over them, the gun now in his hands.

"Mom! Dad!" Nora shouted. Winston and Debra looked up at Chase, scrambled backwards, following Nora. Chase took aim.

He pulled the trigger, and the back of the man's head ruptured outward onto the street. Debra screamed, and Winston cradled her in his arms, talking into her ear, tears sliding down his face.

Chase lowered the gun, stood staring at what the bullet had done to the masked man's head.

A sharply pitched tone whined in Nora's ears. She wasn't sure if it was from the gunshot or the sudden silence. A few seconds passed before she realized she was in the same state as Chase—statued in place, staring.

She stood up and grabbed Chase's arm. "Chase."

He seemed startled, looked back at her.

"Let's go," she said. She turned to Winston and Debra. "Mom. Dad. Let's go."

Her parents helped each other upright.

They all walked back to the SUV, molded themselves into the seats.

Nora's hand quaked with exhausted adrenaline as she reached forward for the keys in the ignition. She started the engine.

"Shit," Chase said. "Nora, go!"

Nora followed his eyes.

The elderly man had reemerged from the building, now holding a bolt-action hunting rifle, cackling maniacally, lifting the gunsight to his right eye.

Nora raked the car into gear and hit the gas pedal hard. The SUV, an old Nissan Pathfinder, roared forward out of the intersection.

The first shot from the rifle made Nora flinch, but missed the vehicle. Her heart drummed. The second bullet exploded a taillight.

They were almost a block away now, and Nora put her hands in position on the wheel to turn left down the next cross street.

The back windshield caved inward, and Nora heard a sickening splatter, felt something like warm paint hit the side of her face. She turned the car down the perpendicular street, out of the elderly man's sightline.

Nora touched the side of her face, confused, stared at her fingers, bright red. She looked to her right. The car became a vacuum, devoid of sound. Chase was slumped forward, his face against the glove compartment, turned toward her, his eyes wide and staring, the top left of his head missing.

Nora felt herself scream, yell his name, though all volume was dialed away. She grabbed the shirt at his shoulder, soaked through with blood, shook him, still screaming, trying to get him to wake up, to blink and look at her with his buttery umber eyes. Hands grabbed her shoulders, gripped her arm, pulling her away from Chase.

Sound flooded back into her awareness.

"Let him go, Nora, honey. Stop shaking him," her mom said.

"I'm sorry, Nora, he's gone. We have to keep going," her dad said. "We have to get further away from that guy. You have to focus on driving, or let me drive."

Nora turned to look through the front windshield. The SUV had slowed to almost a complete stop, her foot off the gas pedal, coasting down the center of the road, listing slightly to the left.

Xavier

Just past Ottawa, heading southwest toward Toronto, the temperature reader on the dashboard of the Jeep Compass ticked up to 158 degrees Fahrenheit. Xavier tracked the numbers carefully, glancing down from the road every few seconds. In this heat, he thought, the reader might not be operating properly, which meant the outside temperature could be hotter. He had less than a five hour drive left to the closest clear zone, a zone that encapsulated a small town just outside Toronto, and he was competing against the onslaught of a severe heat spell, the land around him dried, the distance a shimmering mirage in all directions. To the northwest, rampant wildfires had spread deep orange across the sky, smoke screening the sun into a perfect circle. Within two days time, the heat in this region would be well over 200 degrees.

Xavier lifted the map, which was folded to show the current route, from the passenger seat. The map was littered with notes and highlighted roads, street names and highway numbers, timelines and degrees of longitude and latitude. The beginnings of directions for the Minneapolis clear zone had been crossed out, scratched from his options when he realized it wasn't reachable by the schedule. He had been hoping to begin moving further south, which had its own package of problems, but where the temperatures were slightly milder.

He was fortunate, he thought, that the Compass was a newer model, built after manufacturers had begun making more heat resistant vehicles due to the acceleration of global warming, when record high temperatures in some areas had crept over 140 degrees Fahrenheit. He still remembered the news footage of fish floating dead in rivers.

Xavier slowed the car as he approached a crossroads, looked down at the map, back up to survey each corner for a road sign. He saw no standing sign, though he recognized the distant rectangular glint of metal about forty yards out from the nearest point of road, what he assumed was the back of the sign he was hunting. He looked over his shoulder, at his brother, Whitman, sleeping in the backseat.

"Whit, wake up," Xavier said.

Whitman swiped a hand at the back of the passenger seat and rolled over.

"Whit, wake the hell up!"

Whitman growled, sat upright, wiping a hand across his face. "Fuck, what, X?"

"There's a road sign down. We need to know what it says." Xavier motioned with his head.

Whitman squinted, staring out into the dirt field. "So what? Let's go check it."

"The temperature."

Whitman looked at the dashboard. "Shit."

"Yeah. And we don't have time to double-back at the next road. Engine's in the red."

"Well, what's the plan then?"

Xavier unbuckled his seatbelt. "I'll go check it. You stay here. Pass me that blanket from the floor back there." He pulled the car next to a small man-sized gap in the concrete barrier that ran the length of the road closest to the sign, shifted the engine into park and let it idle.

Whitman handed him the yellow wool blanket. "Blanket? With the heat?"

"To keep the direct sunlight off me," Xavier said, opening the front seat's center compartment for the work gloves inside.

Whitman looked outside, back down to the dash. "How the hell hot is that going to be?"

"I don't know." Xavier pulled on each glove. "We'll see." He hooded the blanket over his head. "If it ends up being too hot and I don't make it back, you'll have your own decision to make. Take this turn or head to the next one." He looked at his brother in the rearview. "But I'll make it back."

"X, look, maybe…"

Xavier opened the door and stepped out of the car.

The heat almost knocked him back into his seat, surprising despite his bracing, something he had to immediately rebalance and push himself through. He picked himself up into a run, sweat immediately on his arms, driving down his legs and dampening the blanket around his forehead. Breathing seared his throat, his lungs aching with each heave. His mind became light about halfway to the sign, the fiery landscape shifting and tilting around him. Sweat began to fall into his vision from the top edge of the blanket like raining crystals.

When he reached the sign, Xavier picked it up, dropped it from the shock of its heat through the gloves, bent low and flipped it quickly. The shining white letters swam in front of him. He turned and raised a thumb up toward the Jeep Compass, signaling to Whitman that it was the correct road sign. Xavier put his head down and started the sprint back to the car, his eyes following his feet, each step's munching scrape into dirt. He looked up. The car seemed as if it was further than it had been before. He lowered his head and kept running. Darkness floated into his periphery, blackening the edges of his sight, until all he could see was the splitting seams of his Nikes.

#

Xavier opened his eyes with a gasp, his vision a slowing spin, the windows of the car twirling around him. His shirt and shorts were sopping. He was lying across the backseat.

"Drink," Whitman said from the driver's seat.

"What?" Xavier's brain tried to grip his surroundings to a

standstill. He felt like he was on a carousel.

"Drink. The water. On the floor next to you."

Xavier looked down at the plastic jug of water on the floor of the backseat. "What happened?"

"You collapsed right as you reached the wall. I dragged your ass back into the car. Got a little toasted myself."

"Shit. I don't even remember."

"Yeah, I poured a bunch of our water on you to cool you down. I thought you were going to fucking die of heatstroke." Whitman shook his head. "You were unconscious for like twenty minutes."

Xavier was almost too weak to lift the gallon jug to his lips, but managed to swallow a mouthful of the water. He looked out at the moving landscape through the window. "Did you make the turn?"

"Yeah, I made the turn," Whitman said. He looked at Xavier in the rearview. "How does your face feel?"

"What?" The right side of Xavier's face began to burn, as if surging back into his reality.

Almost all the skin on his body stung as he turned in his seat, though the pain on his face was the most alarming. He leaned his head to look at himself in the rearview mirror.

The left side of his face was a sunburnt shade of red. The right side, from the top of his forehead to his jawline, was a deep ruby mass of blood and unburied skin, the flesh under flesh, and though it had been doused with water, there were still remnants of dirt and tiny pebbles imbedded in their self-secured cavities. Xavier winced as he turned his face back and forth to assess the damage.

"Shit," he said.

"Yeah, you took a bad dive when you blacked out. You were running pretty fast. A few more feet and you would have hit the barrier. So, could have been worse." Whitman spoke over his shoulder. "Hey, ladies dig scars, right?"

Nausea crept into Xavier's gut. "I think I'm going to be sick."

"I'd be surprised if you didn't." Whitman grabbed the blanket from the passenger seat and dropped it on the floor of the back. "If you're going to puke, do it in the blanket. We can toss it out the window or something."

Xavier drank more water, poured a bit over his face, inhaling sharply through clasped teeth biting into themselves from the burn. "I think I'll be okay."

"Yeah." Whitman spoke over his shoulder again. "Yeah, you'll be okay, brother. And we only have about four hours before we reach Orangeville." He paused. "Hey, you remember that hangover cure you use to make?"

"What?"

"That hangover cure, what was it? Ah, a glass of Alka-Seltzer and one of those berry energy shots. Remember? What'd you use to call it?"

"Reverse boilermaker."

"That's right! A reverse boilermaker." Whitman slapped his palm against the steering wheel.

"Worked every time," Xavier said.

"Bet you could use one of those right now, huh?"

Despite the pain and nausea, Xavier laughed.

#

When Xavier saw the cardinal as they drove into a residential neighborhood of Orangeville, Canada, he thought he was hallucinating. The bird, a brilliant, almost illuminant red, was resting on the flag of a mailbox that had been torn from the ground and dropped onto a driveway.

Whitman was looking at the dashboard. "Yes! We're under a hundred degrees now. 97. X, take a look."

"Do you see that?" Xavier said.

"See what?"

"The bird. Slow down. It's a cardinal."

Whitman looked to where Xavier was pointing. "Oh yeah. I see him. Red son-of-gun, isn't he?"

"Wow."

"Yeah, can't remember last time I saw one of them. Good eye,

X."

Xavier could number the living animals he'd seen in the last year with just his fingers. He wondered how long that cardinal had traveled to get to this place, what it had survived to be resting on that mailbox on this day.

"There, how about that one?" Whitman said, motioning toward a large, mostly intact white house with beige brick siding and a large wooden porch. "Looks pretty good. It's gotta have a basement."

"Sure. Let's check it out."

Whitman pulled into the driveway. "You sure you don't want me to check it out first?"

"Nah, I'm good. I feel much better now."

As Xavier straightened himself up out of the car and closed the door behind him, the 97 degree heat unbalanced him for a moment. He put a hand out onto the hot metal of the Compass' roof, drew his hand away. After a deep breath, he turned toward the house.

"Hey," he said, craning his neck slightly. "There's a side door over there. I'll take that. You go in through the front. Grab the lantern."

"Copy that," Whitman said, turning back toward the trunk for the solar-charged electric lantern.

Xavier moved through the perfectly still air, wishing a breeze would sweeten the sweat already salting his brow. The four wooden steps that led up to the side door of the house, peeling maroon paint, squeaked like dying mice as he scaled them.

He stepped into the dim hush of the house, the door battering against its own jam like a triggered pinball lever, startling him a few feet forward.

He was standing in the kitchen, a kitchen that reminded him of the 1950's family sitcoms he used to watch as a kid while he and Whitman waited for their mother to get home from her late evening shift as a motel front desk clerk. Though now this kitchen was forgotten, a graveyard of dead appliances, light straining through the shutters' slats, Xavier could sense it was once a place of happiness and connection.

Whitman appeared at the kitchen door toward the front of the house, holding up the lit lantern. "There you are." He stomped his foot into the kitchen linoleum. "Oh yeah, this place definitely has a basement. I can feel it."

Xavier raised an open palm. "Stop." He listened, heard silence. "There goes why we've been so quiet this entire time."

"Ah, come on. Nobody's here. Now let's find these stairs and get you down to where it's cooler." Whitman stepped out of the kitchen, looked up the hallway. "Ah." He disappeared from the kitchen entrance.

Xavier followed him. The hallway had thick beige carpet, yellowing white walls, and a musty odor. At the far end, Whitman opened a door and looked down.

"Yup," Whitman said. "Bingo." He looked at Xavier and jerked his head toward the stairs before descending, the glow of the lantern traveling with him.

Xavier walked the hall and looked down into the darkness past the lantern's light, started down towards it, a few steps behind Whitman. As he reached the bottom of the stairs, a voice ricocheted against the cement floor of the unfinished basement.

"Don't move! Don't you move! I have a gun!" The voice was male and shaky. A light from a portable lamp lit up part of the basement to the right and behind the bottom of the stairs, revealing a man and a woman, early thirties, both wearing worn shorts and dingy T-shirts. Despite their drab appearance, they were a handsome pair. They crouched with their backs to the corner of the room.

"Whoa, whoa! Easy there. We come in peace," Xavier said.

"Like hell," the woman yelled.

"Look at us. We're not armed," Whitman said. "We're just looking for shelter." He pointed at Xavier. "This is—he's my brother. He almost died from the heat earlier today. He needs rest. Look at him. He needs someplace cool. That's all."

The man pressed the gun forward in the air. "Yeah, well, how are we supposed to trust you?" The gun was cylinder chambered, medium caliber.

"I get it. We both do," Whitman said, looking at his brother. "We've had our fair share of unpleasant run-ins. But we have water, up in our car, and we have some canned food. We'd be more than willing to share."

The man gave a side glance toward the woman next to him. "Well, we have water. But we're very short on food."

"There, you see? Let us help. We were just checking out the place first, but we can go up and get the food now. Okay? Sound good?" Whitman raised his hands, the lantern still dangling from one of them.

"I don't know," the man said.

Xavier took a quick survey of what he could see in the basement, a long room with a low ceiling, under seven feet tall, with two doorless entries to side rooms along its right wall.

"Well, you just have to go with your gut. That's my philosophy," Whitman said. "If you're not okay with this, we'll just be on our way, okay?" He started backing toward the stairs.

"No, wait," the man said. He lowered the revolver.

With one unbroken motion, Xavier drew a 10mm pistol from the back of his belt, tucked under his shirt, brought it around and shot the man in the forehead above his left eye. Blood hit the walls, some spattering the face of the woman, who turned toward the man enough to catch the second bullet in her left temple. They dropped to the floor, shoulder to shoulder, almost simultaneously. Xavier lowered the gun.

"You said you were going to let me get the next ones," Whitman said.

"Next time, be faster," Xavier said. "Now help me with the bodies, then we can go through their inventory. We need to get them good and far from the house. With the heat out there, they'll cook up a stench quickly."

"Copy that," Whitman said. He walked around Xavier, who had already picked up the man's hands. Whitman bent down to lift the man's feet.

"Wait," Xavier said. "Wait, did you hear that?"

"Hear what?" Whitman said, though in the next moment he heard it too.

Echoing from one of the basement's side rooms was the sound of an infant crying.

Marlene and Bartley

The sun's downward climb in the sky cast shade across the interior of the one-story dental office, the roof of which had long been ripped from its supporting walls. The walls remained upright and solid, providing cover from the street's open angles, and Marlene stepped within them to shield herself from those sight lines. After days of walking, favoring a severely sprained ankle, she was tempted to collapse a few feet past the entrance, in what was once the office's waiting room, among cheap red-cushioned chairs flipped and scattered, cushions water-warped and moldy, faint traces of dissolving magazine covers littering the floor, but she inhaled full and slow, and stirred the energy to keep moving, knowing she should get deeper into the building before resting.

Since arriving in Minneapolis, Marlene had been scaling through the city blocks, scavenging for food, water, a working car and radio. Her search was unsuccessful, and her pack carrying the food and water she had managed to salvage from the Mazda was getting excruciatingly light.

As she walked through the interior waiting room door, her left hiking shoe left a footprint in the powdered plaster residue on a fallen **Please Wear a Mask** sign. She twisted past the debris in the main hallway—dislocated dental chairs and X-ray machines—and turned into the last examination room at the far end.

"Whoa!" a man shouted. He was sitting bunched up in the corner of the room, a backpack next to him, right leg bent, knee up, his hand gripping the shin, the other leg stretched out flat, a makeshift tourniquet wrapping his left thigh, soaked through with blood. He held up his left hand. "Whoa! Hey, I don't have anything!"

Marlene screamed in surprise. Her first instinct was to run, but something struck her about the man's words: *I don't have anything.*

An ugly laceration divided his forehead into horizontal halves. Traces of dried blood dusted his beard. His skin was a grayish white. He grimaced as he shifted his bodyweight.

"What do you mean you don't have anything?" Marlene said.

"I don't have anything. Nothing of value. Please." The man seemed exhausted, on the verge of losing consciousness.

"I'm not going to take anything from you."

The man hesitated, stared at her face for an extended moment. His shoulders relaxed. "Thank you," he said. There was a kindness in his eyes that Marlene found disarming.

"Are you okay?" she said.

"I… I don't know."

"You look like you're in pretty rough shape." Marlene put a hand on her chest. "I am—was—a nurse. Can I help you?"

He shrugged pessimistically. "You can try."

"I have a first aid kit in my bag. Not much in it, but I think I can dress some of those wounds. Keep them from getting infected."

The man looked at her with a flash of confusion, as if he hadn't been offered help in the entirety of his lifetime. "Thank you."

Marlene stepped over a dental table that was lying on its side, lowered herself to her knees next to him. She chicken-winged her bag from her shoulder, removed the first aid kit, a small metal wall unit she found in a West Virginia Costco. She opened the kit and grabbed gauze wrap and alcohol wipes, and began dabbing the man's forehead with one of the wipes. His expression tightened.

"So what's your name?" she said. Idle talk helped distract

patients from pain.

"Bartley," the man said.

"Bartley. I like that name. I'm Marlene."

"A pleasure," Bartley said.

#

Bartley cranked the handle on the can opener, opening the first of the two cans of baked beans he had pulled from his pack. He placed the can in front of Marlene, who was sitting next to him against the wall. He began opening the second can.

"Wow, baked beans with real bits of bacon," Marlene said. She gave Bartley a side glance. "I thought you said you didn't have anything of value."

Bartley handed her a plastic spoon. "I lied," he said. He placed a hand on the fresh bandaging around his thigh. "It's the least I can do."

Marlene swallowed a spoonful of beans—savory and sweet. "So, if you don't mind my asking. How'd you get those injuries?"

Bartley spoke around a bite. "Long story short, I ran into some pirates. They wanted what I had." He seemed to lose himself in memory, stared vacantly at the floor, stopped chewing.

"And you got away." Marlene said.

"And I got away." Bartley nodded.

"How long have you been traveling alone?"

"Since the beginning. How about you?"

The plastic spoon drooped in Marlene's grip. Bartley sensed that she regretted asking the question as soon as it was reciprocated.

"Look, you don't have to…" he said.

"It's okay," she said. "I just… I had been traveling with my husband. Well, he was my ex-husband. We were on our way here, to Minneapolis." Her eyes moved as she stared at the air in front of her, as if she was seeing a movie screen invisible to Bartley. "We ran behind schedule." Her eyebrows moved inward. "We were so close. The storm, our car was literally thrown from it, into the clear zone. The way we landed, upside-down on the driver's side. His head," she paused, "Jackson's head was…" A tear snapped loose from her left eye, another from her right. She put down the can and wiped her cheeks with with her palms. "At least it was fast. Had to have been painless." She looked down at her foot. "And me, just a sprained ankle. How does that happen?"

Bartley had stopped eating too, was watching her intently. He looked away, down into his can of beans. "I'm sorry," he said.

"Yeah," she said. "Seems like the world is nothing but sorries these days."

"That must have been just, what, four days ago?"

Marlene nodded. "Something like that. Fucked up thing is," she hesitated, inhaled short and sharp. "I'm pregnant."

Bartley's eyes snapped up to her face, back down to the floor. Both of them were, for a moment, silent. "Congratulations," he said.

"Yeah, thanks."

"Do you have a car, a vehicle of some kind?"

"No, I've been looking for one, but…"

"Radio?"

"No." She motioned with her hand. "We used the car's."

Bartley looked at her again, a realization breaking through him.

"Well," he said. "My motorcycle can seat two. Won't be very comfortable, but it'll get us to the next clear zone. I have a radio. I think we should travel together for a while, if you'd like. At least until you find a car and build your supplies back up. What do you think?"

Marlene didn't look at him, but another tear fell from her face. "Thank you," she said.

#

Bartley was scraping the last bit of beans from the bottom of the can when he heard a woman's shout—loud, coming from outside the dental office, to the southwest—followed by a full-throated scream. He was on his feet before his mind caught up. He bent down and removed his nightstick from his pack.

"Wait," Marlene said. She stood up next to him. "What are you doing?"

"Stay here," he said.

"No. Don't." Her head quaked side to side. "It could be a trap."

Bartley looked at her. "You weren't a trap." He turned toward the examination room door. "Stay here."

As he stepped into the hallway, another scream. He faced the end of the hall, saw an emergency exit a few yards away, ran to it. The door opened into a side alley, shadow-spilt by twilight. Bartley looked to his right, toward the street. A woman with white-blonde hair ran across the mouth of the alley.

"Hey!" Bartley shouted.

The woman slowed, turned toward him. Even in the low light, Bartley could see the desperation stamped into her features. She was older than he expected, maybe late fifties or early sixties. She wore a sleeveless salmon shirt and white shorts.

"You okay?" he said.

She looked back in the direction she was running from, started jogging into the alley. "They're after me!" she shouted. "Four of them!"

"Come on!" Bartley motioned her toward the door. "Get inside. I'm a friend."

He held the door open as she entered the building. As Bartley stepped inside after her, he glimpsed the first of her pursuers, a man with a clean-shaven face, turning the corner into the alley. He was at a full run, wore a collared polo shirt and jeans, normal in appearance save the madness in his face and the handgun tucked into his waistline.

Bartley yanked the emergency door closed. Marlene was out in the hallway now, her hands on the other woman's shoulders, keeping her steady. The woman heaved with panicked breaths.

"You two, go. Get in that room. Three doors down. Put whatever you can behind the door once you're in there."

"Bartley…" Marlene said.

"Go!"

The emergency door began to open. The gun came through first, raised, pointer finger on the trigger. Bartley sidestepped, swung the nightstick down into the wrist, breaking it. The gun rattled across the hallway, slid up against a pile of debris. The man yelled and cradled his wrist with his other hand. Bartley reached through the exit and grabbed the man's collar, pulling him into the building, smacking him on the back of the head with the nightstick as he did. The man's skull cracked audibly, and he slammed into the ground with dead weight, squeaking across the tile. His torso twitched involuntarily. Bartley reached out and closed the exit door again.

Both women were still in the hallway, looking from Bartley to the man's body.

Bartley walked to the man's gun, a Beretta, picked it up, checking the safety. "Get in the room," he said. "Barricade the door."

The two women vanished into the examination room and shut the door.

Bartley walked backward through the hallway, keeping the gun aimed at the emergency exit. As he moved, he knelt down and plucked a dental tray from the floor, grimacing as the newly dressed wound in his thigh stretched. He continued moving backward until he reached the door to the waiting room. Without looking, he lowered himself to place the metal tray leaning upright against the closed door and the doorjamb. He straightened, and began to slowly walk forward.

As soon as the emergency exit opened, Bartley began firing. The man rushing through the door—taller than the last one, much thinner, carrying a 12 gauge pump shotgun—took two bullets in the chest, one in the shoulder. Bartley dropped to a knee, fired three more shots, all misses, two when the man was already going to the ground.

Bartley heard the metal tray hit tile. He threw himself onto his back, firing upside down toward the waiting room door. The upside down figure running toward him triggered a pair of shots from a handgun before he fell to the floor, the two bullets cutting the air less than a foot above Bartley, who kept firing, the words *four of them* repeating in his mind. The trigger clicked three times past the gun being empty.

Bartley sat up, glancing both ways down the hall, calculating which gun was closest.

"Stop!" Another figured appeared at the waiting room doorway, the fourth man, holding a 357 magnum revolver. "You son of a bitch."

He was wearing a white button-up shirt and corduroy pants, his face shaved clean.

Bartley, still on the ground, pivoted to face him, and began slowly sliding himself backwards.

The man advanced on him. "I said don't fucking move!"

Bartley didn't have a choice. He continued moving backward toward the shotgun. The man moved faster, and soon stood within a few feet from Bartley, the giant revolver leveled downward at him. Bartley stopped moving.

"You killed my friends," the man said.

"Was them or me." Bartley was still too far from the shotgun, and the man stood a foot beyond kicking range.

"Well, now it is you, hero." The man shifted his aim from Bartley's chest to his head.

The examination room door three doors down from the exit, the door directly to the pirate's right, swung open hard, catching the long barrel of the revolver, driving it downward, a shot ringing the air, the bullet going through the door and into the tile. The door's followthrough connected with the man's face, breaking his nose and sending him to the floor on his back. Marlene came around the door, screaming, a pair of dental scissors gripped in her right hand. She dove on top of the stunned man and drove the scissors into his neck.

Bartley rolled backward, tore the shotgun from dead hands. He rose to both knees, the shotgun trained down the hall.

The man kicked Marlene off of him, scissors still in his neck, blood running down into his shirt. She hit the wall on the right side of the hallway.

Bartley, knowing the shotgun's spread, aimed toward the left side of the hall, and fired. The buckshot riddled the man's right side, tearing through his arm and part of his face as he attempted to stand. He went to the ground again.

Bartley stood from his knees. "Marlene, get back!" he said.

Marlene stepped backward, past Bartley.

With the sightline clear, Bartley pumped the shotgun, fired, pumped and fired again. Blood colored the walls and floor around the man's now motionless body.

Bartley yelled, fell sideways into a lean against the left wall. He looked at Marlene, who was squeezing her right shoulder.

"You okay?"

"I think so," she said, looking at him.

"You saved us," he said.

"Returning the favor."

The other woman stepped into the hallway, her eyes absorbing the scene. "I… I can't believe this. I can't believe we're still alive."

Bartley smiled at her weakly. "Believe it," he said.

The woman looked at Bartley, away from the dead bodies strewn through the hallway. "Thank you. Thank you both so much."

Bartley nodded. "What's your name?"

"Tori," she said. "My name is Tori."

Part Two

Sheryl

The midday sun hung like a blinding yoke from the highest angle in the sky, baking the deserted streets of Louisville, Kentucky into a skillet driving heat back upward through the humidity-weighted air among the collapsed red-bricked apartments, eroded sports bars and corner diners, the half caved-in blade of the university stadium spiking in the distance.

Sheryl Dawkins sprinted along the sidewalks through the city, staying in the shade of buildings whenever possible as she attempted to suppress the panic that flared in her chest.

"Bruce!" she shouted. "Bruce!"

At every corner, she stopped and looked anxiously in all directions.

The high rattle of cicadas pulsed from the backdrop around her. Recently, she had found comfort in that sound. To her, it was a reminder that something else was surviving this world. It represented life. Now, it intensified her fear for the life currently in jeopardy. The bonfire scent gusting down from the fires to the north had a similar effect. What usually would have stirred nostalgia within her, now made her more frantic to find the dog that used to croissant at her feet during backyard nights around the blaze in her fire pit.

"Bruce!"

Sheryl stopped when she heard the jingle of Bruce's collar. She held herself still, keenly listening.

"You okay?" said a voice behind her.

Sheryl jumped, spun to face a man standing in front of the soot-covered barbershop she had just passed, its door closing behind him with a quiet jingle of small bells tied to its lock. The man wore a sleeveless undershirt, revealing tanned skin completely wrapped in tattoos—skulls and dragons, the top of a red-inked heart peeking out from the low collar. The tattoos continued around his legs, below basketball shorts with two orange stripes down each side. He was thin, wiry thin, collar bones clearly defined in their protuberance, mimicking the bones that were inked on them. His face was gaunt and grizzled, and there was a noticeable concave along his right jawline. His hair was shoulder-length and greasy, and fell from underneath a soiled San Francisco 49ers cap that looked as if it had been dropped into a car engine. A large military pack was pulling heavily at his back, an assault rifle slung across it. His eyebrows lifted, his eyes blue as the windowsill hydrangeas she could vaguely remember.

Sheryl felt the pearls of sweat on her face multiply. Her heart, already quickened by her running, now beat in her temples. She took a step backward.

"Hey, I'm not going to hurt you," the man said. "You looking for someone?"

Sheryl shook her head.

"Bruce. I heard you yelling. Look, I can help if you want. Is he your son?"

Sheryl took another step backward.

"Look, you can turn and go, and I ain't going to chase you. All I'm saying is I'm willing to help."

Sheryl stammered slightly as she spoke. "It's my dog."

"Aw, shit. He's around here somewhere though?"

She nodded. Her eyes moved from his dingy Reeboks to his face.

"Ma'am, I ain't going to hurt you. I ain't that tough. That's what the tattoos are for."

"He ran off. About ten minutes ago. Like he was chasing something I couldn't see."

"Yeah, well, sounds like a dog to me. I'll help you look for him. First things first, though—I'm Cole." When he saw her shoulders stiffen, he added. "Don't worry, you ain't got to shake my hand or nothing. You can keep your distance if you'd like. I won't take it personal."

"I'm Sheryl," she said.

"Pleased to meet you, Sheryl. Now, let's find this rascal of yours."

"He was headed up this way," she motioned, "toward the highway."

The wildfires burned just beyond the highway and the Ohio River, and were traveling east.

"Yeah, well, it's still a ways off. If he stops to sniff around, we'll catch up to him before he gets that far. We should spread out a bit though, take parallel streets to widen our net best we can."

"Okay."

"I'll go one street over. We'll move at a steady pace, make visual contact every two intersections before moving forward. Just give a holler if you spot him. You need water?"

She shook her head, gestured to the backpack strapped to her shoulders. "No, but we have to hurry. The radio gave an adjustment."

Cole's eyes snapped to her. "What? An adjustment? I haven't turned on my radio today."

"There's a flood coming up from the south, from the hurricane down there. We have to find high ground, at least twenty-five feet above ground-level. It's supposed to start just after midnight tonight."

Cole's eyebrows came together; his chin flexed. "Shit," he said. "Okay, well, let's find your dog. Then we'll find that high ground."

"Thank you," Sheryl said.

"No, ma'am." He looked at her. "Thank you." He pulled at his pack's strap that ran diagonal across his chest, and jogged away toward the parallel street. He stopped halfway up the block, turned back. "If you have a car with anything you need in it… the flooding will wipe it out."

"I don't," she said.

Cole nodded. "Okay." He crossed the remaining distance to the next street and vanished around the corner.

She began to move, a steady jog, her shoes abraded by pavement.

"Bruce!" She heard Cole's voice in the distance.

Every two intersections, she saw him standing at his intersection's center, amongst charred cars or fallen streetlights, waiting for her. As soon as she entered his view, he was gone. This repeated for six blocks before he was missing from their visual check-in. She swallowed, her throat strained from dryness.

"Cole!" she shouted, then stopped herself from shouting again. If Cole had run into trouble, she didn't want to summon that trouble toward her.

She walked slowly up the block toward the intersection, breathing the hot Kentucky oxygen, sweat streaming past her ears. A deathly silence throttled her senses, until it was gradually broken by an excited voice, and the jingle of a dog's tags.

As she neared the lefthand corner of the intersection she could distinguish the voice's words: "Oh, yeah, that's a good boy. Who's a good dog? That's right. You're a good dog."

She turned the corner to see Bruce leaping at Cole's face, tongue lapping, while Cole scratched the rambunctious German shepherd's back and sides voraciously.

"You found him!" she said.

"More like he found me," Cole said, still wrestling with Bruce. "Didn't you? Didn't you, boy?"

"Thank you so much, Cole."

Cole stood, his hands still sparring playfully with Bruce, who danced around his legs. "No worries," he said. "But now we have to find a safe elevation—if you want to stick together until after the flood hits."

"Sure," she said. "At least until after the flood."

He looked at her. "I have a car, but I haven't seen any standing parking garages or anything like that around here, so I doubt we'll be able to save it. Has little left in the tank anyway."

"Yeah, my Kia ran out of gas about seven miles from this clear zone. Bruce and I had to hike the rest of the way in. We barely made it in time."

"I barely made it out of Minneapolis," Cole said, leaning down to scratch Bruce between the eyes. "So we survive the flood, then see what's left."

Survive and scavenge, Sheryl thought. *As always.*

Cole looked at the sky. "We should get started. That stadium off over there has the height, but looks like it's standing by a thread. Again, no parking structures. That means that we're looking for a two-story house or an office building that can clear 25 feet above ground. Right?"

Sheryl nodded. "Right."

"The higher the better." He squinted up the street—nothing but glare and silhouettes from Sheryl's perspective. "Let's head that direction. I'm pretty sure it's the business district. We can backtrack to my car and use what's left of its tank for a faster search."

"Okay. I trust you," she said, surprised by her words.

#

"You smoke?" Cole asked, holding out a pack of cigarettes with a few protruding from the opened casing. He and Sheryl sat on the roof of a three-story Louisville office building, both of them leaning back against the rear of the outcropping that allowed access to the top of the interior stairwell. Bruce was leashed to a metal pole a few yards away, coiled, sleeping.

Sheryl shook her head. "No, but thanks."

"No problem," Cole said. He whipped a cigarette to his mouth and lit the end with a Zippo colored like an American flag. "Military got me started on these. Always promised my mom I wouldn't, but hell has a way of breaking your resolve, and it was hell over there. Especially after the redeployment. It was even worse after that. Much, much worse after that. Cigarettes were the things least trying to kill us." He gestured toward the golfball-sized chunk missing from his jawline, noticeable even through the grizzle of his beard. "That's how I got this beauty. Caught a fragment from a landmine that was thirty yards away."

Sheryl was watching his face, which seemed overly weathered for a man she assumed was in his early thirties. Her eyebrows were steepled with sympathy, with imagining. "I'm sorry," was all that she could think to say.

"Ah, bunch of other guys got it worse that day. The thing is, the technology we had back then, they could have fixed it. My face, I mean. Could have fixed me right up. Some reconstructive surgery, and it would have been almost like it never happened." He exhaled smoke. "But the army wouldn't pay for it. They called it 'cosmetic.'"

"That's terrible," Sheryl said. Cole looked at her. "Not the way it looks. I mean it's terrible that they wouldn't pay for it."

Cole smiled. "I knew what you meant." He paused for a few seconds. "Then I was shipped back to the states, and that's when the drugs started. The pain and the drugs. Funny how that works. They had no problem writing prescriptions. Like damn poets writing haiku or something."

"Fentanyl?" Sheryl said.

Cole gave a short nod. "That's how it started. Then the next miracle drug hit the market. Then the next. All supposedly more effective and less addictive than the last. At the end, before my rehab, I was full-blown addicted to Dexamethalin."

"I've heard of that."

"Similar effect to an opioid, only more potent, and with a raging kick of adrenaline—like doing a line of meth and a hit of heroin all at once. One hit gets you addicted, and there's only a 4 percent recovery rate. And that was for the people who even attempted rehabilitation. So again, I guess I'm lucky."

He reached for his pack, lying next to him. "Can I show you something?"

"Sure." Sheryl spoke with hesitation.

"Don't worry," Cole said. He pulled from his pack a large plastic bag full of small white pills, circles with tiny print engraved into them. The bag was about the size of a brick, stuffed to its seams.

"This," Cole said, "is Dexamethalin."

"Cole..."

"Collected it from a pharmacy a couple years ago. Carried it on me ever since."

"Are you sure you should have that?" Sheryl leaned forward, a compressed nausea in her stomach.

"Helps keep me humble. For some reason, it's comforting knowing it's there, and it's reassuring to know the ol' willpower is still strong—my conviction in my sobriety." He shrugged. "And if my situation ever becomes hopeless," he held up the bag, "this will be a hell of a send-off."

Sheryl leaned back against the wall. "Shit," she said. "That's a hell of a thing."

"Yeah, well. We should eat." He placed the bag of pills back in his pack and dug out a few cans. "I'm down to just vegetables, but at least it's something. Creamed corn or asparagus spears?"

"You don't have to."

"Look, if it weren't for you, I'd be on my way to drowning. Now, creamed corn or asparagus spears?"

She smiled. "Spears."

He set the can down next to her, along with a can opener. "Have at it."

She cranked the lid off the asparagus, crunched one between her teeth. "You know," she looked up at the darkening sky. "I used to be so obsessed with my age. *Obsessed.* After I turned thirty, it became like a reminder of my mortality. That I was growing closer to death."

"That happens for a lot of people," Cole said.

"Yeah, but I mean, it was bad with me. Like, it made me miserable. I did whatever I could to avoid birthdays or those pesky numbers on my driver's license. I tried to hide it from everyone."

Cole looked at her.

"But now..." She shook her head. "I was forty-four years old when the world went to hell. Just scrambling to survive, I lost track of time. Now, I have no idea how old I am. Not my exact age, anyway." She gave a short laugh, "I should be happy, right? Now, when someone asks my age, I can just say 'unknown.' But I can't help finding myself wanting to know. Like it's a part of my identity that I lost."

Cole smiled. "I can understand that. And for the record, you don't look a day over 'unknown.'"

Sheryl laughed.

"Sometimes people focus on the wrong things," Cole said. "It's human. We obsess and obsess until something shows us where our true focus should be. I mean, even in these times. We're all so focused on surviving that we've lost sight of what we're surviving for. This life, it's not about the disasters, not about the storms or the earthquakes or the floods. It's about what happens in the places between them. We still have to find moments to live."

"Like now," Sheryl said.

"Yes, like now."

Sheryl snapped down on another spear. "You know, I never knew how delicious canned asparagus spears are."

Cole looked at her and laughed. He flicked his finished cigarette, a high-arcing parabola of glowing cherry in the twilight.

\#

A whimper from Bruce woke Sheryl to the view of the low, dark cityscape around her. She could barely discern the shape of Cole standing at the roof's ledge.

"Cole?" she said.

"It's starting," Cole said.

Sheryl stood up, glanced upward at the night sky. The number of visible stars and their enhanced brilliance in the absence of the constant competition from civilization's electric pulse still amazed her. As she crossed the distance to Cole, Bruce barked from his post. She quarter-turned toward him.

"Easy, Bruce. It's okay," she said.

As she stepped next to Cole, she looked down over the ledge. In the moonlight, her eyes adjusting, she could see the flow of dark water on the streets, rippling between buildings, like a shallow tide pushing its way through the city. Within a few seconds, it had risen to the height of car windows, and the wrecked and burnt cars along the street began to turn slowly in its drag. Half a minute later, the cars were floating freely through the streets. Sheryl could now hear the movement of the water.

"You know," Cole said, staring out at the water. "It gets more and more impossible. I mean—gas, supplies…" He waved a hand at everything below. "With the ARWS's adjustment, who's going to survive this?" His voice was strained, defeated.

"We are," Sheryl said.

The water had now buried the first floor of the office building across from them.

Cole looked at her, back out toward the city. "I wasn't a good person, you know," he said. "Especially when I was using. And especially when I was over there. I wasn't a good person at all."

Sheryl looked at him. "Hey," she said, "ever since all this started, I've been looking for anything good that could possibly come from it. Anything good to hold on to." Cole looked at her. She leaned into their meeting gaze. "You're the first good thing, Cole. Don't lose that."

He gave a small nod and looked back out into the city. "Shit."

Sheryl heard it before she saw it, a sound like brick and metal being torn apart, a large black swell rolling in from the distance, three stories high, crashing through the buildings over the surface of the lower water.

There was no hesitation in the panic that immediately raked through her. "Oh shit, that's too high! Shit, that's too high, Cole! That's too high!"

Bruce barked in a frenzy.

Cole watched for a second more. "Yeah, that's too high," he said. He turned and scanned the rooftop, looked at Sheryl. "Get up there! Quick!" He pointed to the stairwell's outcropping. "Use that box to the left. I'll get Bruce."

Sheryl looked to where he was pointing, saw a large metal box against the left wall of the structure, what she assumed was casing for some type of wiring. She ran to the box, stepped onto it and pulled herself onto the top of the outcropping, which by her estimation was maybe seven or eight square feet in surface area. When she turned around, Cole was already lifting Bruce up to her. Bruce was limp in his grasp, ears folded back. She grabbed at his torso, the weight of the dog almost yanking her off the outcropping.

The swell reached the lip of their building, smashed against the ledge with the force of a tsunami, exploding into a shower of heavy cold water. More water surged through behind it, and Cole was swept from his feet, just as Sheryl regained her balance and dropped backward onto the outcropping with Bruce in her arms.

She laid Bruce down and looked back over the edge for Cole, yelling, "Stay, Bruce! Stay!" the roar of the water smothering her voice.

Cole was gone. All she could see was the dark surging current.

Bruce yelped, and Sheryl turned back to him.

"It's okay, Bruce. It's okay." She clutched the dog and spoke low into his ear.

The rush of water was just a foot or two below their platform now, debris clattering and banging against the edge. Suddenly spooked, Bruce unexpectedly twisted in her arms, trying to wrestle free, barking in spasms. Sheryl managed to hold on for a moment, but was unprepared for the fight. Bruce whipped himself away from her body and launched himself off of the outcropping, into the dark water.

"Bruce!" Sheryl yelled, her voice cracked with desperation, her face wet with tears and filthy muddy water. "Bruce!"

She heard two faint barks, the second more distant than the first, then nothing except water.

Sheryl screamed, standing in soaked clothing, eyes closed, torrents of water swarming and slamming around her. She screamed and screamed again.

The water pulled at her ankles, and she was brushed from the outcropping.

For seemingly endless minutes, she tried furiously to swim, but she was whirling in the invading water, her body turning hypothermic, and she had no sense of which direction she was swimming.

Then, something sharp and heavy struck the top of her head, and she felt all the hunger to fight leave her body, a black cloud blooming in the water around her.

Cole

Cole bopped his head, his foot tapping four-times the beat of the music turned up from the battery-powered boombox resting a yard and a half away, Metallica's "Enter Sandman" spinning in its compact disc slot, filling the emptiness of the southeast Michigan evening. Cole stilled his movement, his hand gripping the ink gun pressed from one palm into the other, the left palm being one of the few tattoo-vacant spaces left on his body. An eye, open, almost complete, veins forking through the white of it, stared up at him, his fingers like waving hair above it when he wiggled them. He sat, sporadically screaming along with the lyrics, in a folding chair a few feet from his two-person tent. A bag of pills, almost full, white circles with small print, rested on the ground next to his left foot.

He pressed the last detail, the corner of the eye, the tear duct, into his skin, wiped the blood to see his work, and tossed the ink gun into the grass. He stood up, his head rocking wildly again, his knees kicking up to the music, his shirtless torso gleaming with ink and sweat in the light of his campfire. He yelled, wagged his head, tongue out, his body leaping east and west. He leaned down, laughing, and lifted the bag of pills and a half-full bottle of cheap tequila from the ground, swallowing one of the pills and a finger of the liquor before he dropped both back to the earth, a satisfied growl escaping him. His movement calmed into stillness; he looked into the trees of the surrounding forest, of which he was near the border. He watched the trees in the wavering firelight. He stepped forward, arms widespread, a confronting posture.

"Oh yeah? Make me!" he shouted into the trees. "Make me, you sons-of-bitches! Fucking aye! Fuck you all!"

He turned slightly, aiming his ear in the direction he was shouting, his eyes angling.

He listened, ten seconds, then laughed. "That's what I thought," he said at a normal volume, not even able to hear himself over the music.

Cole walked over to the dead body that lay about fifteen feet from the back of his tent. He had cut the man's throat while scouting a pirate encampment nestled in the outer edge of an industrial container yard about a mile away. This particular pirate had been doing his rounds on guard, patrolling the camp's lightless perimeter. His death had been quick and silent, but not painless.

Cole looked down at the body. "You're starting to smell, dude," he said. "We're going to have to get you a little farther away."

The hammering music and the smell of recently dead flesh reminded him of the first year after the disasters started, when he would hang the skin he peeled from pirates' faces on a clothesline through his camp.

He positioned himself by the man's head, and picked up each arm by the wrist—cold, pulseless. He dragged the man about thirty more yards deeper into the forest before dropping the limbs back into the body. He pulled a pack of Camel Lights from his basketball shorts and lit one with his American flag lighter.

Cole shook the pack of cigarettes at the dead body before pocketing them again. "Thanks for these, by the way. Not my brand, but they'll do."

He walked back to the faded blue folding chair, picking up his SCAR-H assault rifle from its lean against one of the tentpoles on the way, and sat down, squinting from the smoke as he held the cigarette in his teeth. He pulled a rag from the waistband on the left side of his shorts, and began cleaning the rifle. He worked through the process, removing the trigger module, the butt stock and charging handle, next the return spring assembly and bolt carrier, finally disassembling the gas system, meticulously running the cloth through each accessible groove before reassembling the rifle. After he was done, he re-tucked the rag, stood, and lit another cigarette.

He walked over to the parked motorcycle adjacent his tent, and kicked the back tire. The Yamaha YZF-R6's rear tire had gone flat about thirty miles outside the Michigan clear zone, but with no choice, Cole had ridden it the rest of the way in. Even traveling under twenty miles per hour, the metal rim underneath the tire was severely damaged.

While searching the area near where he had settled camp, Cole had discovered the pirate encampment, and while scouting it, saw that they had four large white vans. He planned to steal one, though would wait until a new broadcast came through the radio. He didn't want to spend days stuck in a clear zone while pirates hunted him. And these pirates appeared to be the most ruthless kind; he could smell the death on them.

He had watched as they dragged three captives, two men and a woman, tattered and bloodied, from one of the vans, and forced them to play a game of hot potato with a small stone to blaring rock 'n' roll music. When the music cut out, the captive holding the stone, a man with a bleeding baseball-sized knot on his forehead, was shot in the face before he could utter a sound. The remaining two captives, sobbing and staring at the dead body, were dragged back to the vans.

There were twenty-four pirates by Cole's count—eighteen men, six women—scattered through the large metal shipping containers. Some of them had set up posts and shelters and campfires, some even atop the containers. With the pirates' predictable rotations and positional gaps, Cole had no doubt he'd easily be able to pilfer a van.

As he looked down at the Yamaha, he heard a loud crack issue from the darkness between the trees. His head snapped up, eyes pivoting, his right hand waving away the cigarette smoke around his head. A stillness ensued. Twenty, thirty seconds.

Then two eyes appeared, low, feral, glowing topazes with pupils, twenty-five yards into the forest, reflecting firelight.

Cole calmly took another pull from his cigarette, though his heart picked up its patter, and he slowly un-shouldered his rifle, its barrel swinging upward to aim squarely between the topazes, the stock of the rifle pressed firmly into the bare skin of his shoulder. He bit down on the cigarette's filter, smoke bending by his closed left eye, his right eye aligning down the gun's iron sights.

"Your move," Cole said.

He heard a deep growl. The eyes vanished.

"Good choice." Cole lowered the rifle. He moved back toward the fire, keeping his eyes trained into the trees.

He sat down on the chair by the fire and rested the butt of the rifle's stock against the earth. A cricket stringed out a note. The CD's last track had ended, the disc no longer spinning in its slot, and the boombox had fallen to silence. Cole shook his head hard, as if clearing clouds, and reached for his military pack. Taking another look toward where the yellow eyes had gemmed the darkness, he pulled out his portable Sony radio, and flipped the power switch. The time for directions to a new clear zone was nearing, but only static sounded through the speaker. He lit a fresh cigarette with the final ember of the previous one, and stared into the fire until his eyes burned.

#

Halfway between sleep and consciousness, chin dropped to chest, sweat percolating his forehead, Cole rattled awake to a rustling among the trees—close—darkness curtaining nearer as the fire died down to a smoldering crown. Cole glanced at his rifle, which had slipped from his grip in his stupor, and now lay flat on the ground to his right. He grabbed a stick from a small pile he had stacked next to his chair, poked at the embers with it, then set it on top of them. Light flared for a short moment, then dimmed again as the fresh wood was slow to catch flame. His eyes searched the darkness, and he leaned toward his rifle.

He stopped when he again saw the eyes.

They were closer this time, maybe ten yards away, their owner as hidden as before in the lowered light. For long seconds, there was no sound. Even the insects had halted their song. And no growl came from under the eyes. Cole straightened back up, away from his SCAR-H.

The eyes moved forward, drawing nearer, a shape forming around them, and a dog, a German shepherd, emerged from the night's obfuscation.

Cole's mouth opened involuntarily. "Bruce?"

The German shepherd stopped about five yards away from where Cole sat, a blue collar around its neck, the copper tags glinting in the little light they were able to catch. Cole and the German shepherd stared at each other. Then, the dog whimpered, turned east, to Cole's right, and trotted back into the forest.

"Bruce!" Cole yelled in a whisper. He rapidly picked up his rifle, shouldered it, surveyed his campsite, and headed steadily after the dog.

Cole moved as quickly as he could through the darkness, slightly crouched, his hand out in front of him, blinking, wide-eyed, his pupils adjusting now that they were away from the fire. He caught site of the dog's tail a few times, but mostly he followed by the jingle of the tags. After about ten minutes at this pace, they exited the trees and approached the deserted industrial road that carved through the forest. Dawn began to break a quiet light through the sky, increasing visibility, and Cole could now see the German shepherd, about twenty yards ahead of him, padding across the two-lane paved road.

Cole realized that the dog was headed at an angle to the opposite edge of the forest, where the corner of the container yard was nested along the tree line. The rest of the massive yard branched out toward the road and the horizon and a distant sky split by lightning.

"Bruce!" he said.

The dog's right ear flickered, but the animal did not turn.

Cole followed.

The fencing along the closest perimeter, the south fence line that connected to the east fence, had been plowed flat by storms, leaving the yard easily accessible. The dog was only a football field's length away from the yard now. Some of the containers had been side-turned or toppled by wind velocity, but others still rose in multicolored stacks, creating a presence similar to a fortress as they approached. Some of the containers were aligned perpendicularly with each other, some parallel, the overall arrangement forming a maze of nooks and tunnels, a city of corrugated metal and hidden cover.

The camp was quiet in the early morning hours, but Cole could see a pirate sitting by a fire atop a container near the perimeter, the glow of a cigar at his mouth, and two other pirates walking ground-level among the tents and hulking steel bins.

The German shepherd's paws rattled the leveled chainlink fence as it entered the yard, its toenails clinking against the webbed metal.

Cole followed, unbelieving of his own body's movement, the fence bending beneath his steps. His Reebok's touched dirt, and he was inside the container yard.

The dog turned up the nearest aisle, which ran parallel to the east fence line—containers organized in varying patterns on the left side, and placed in measured intervals along the east fence to the right. Cole could smell metal, fire, decay. He continued down the aisle after the dog.

As he walked, he became aware of figures in his periphery, voices murmuring jokes and disbelief, laughs and the inflection of questions. Cole passed a grouping of tents that was less than twenty yards to his left, saw shadows moving among them. He looked over his shoulder to see that two pirates had stepped into the middle of the aisle behind him, cutting off the possible return route. One had a hockey stick across his shoulders, his wrists resting on it, hands limp. The other had his arms intertwined across his chest, a pistol holstered at his hip.

Cole turned back to the dog, still twenty yards ahead, just as it made a right turn between containers along the eastern fence. Cole kept walking, but a bark echoed through the air, followed by a sharp yelp, and Cole began to run.

His shoes slid to a stop in the dirt as he reached the gap in the containers. He stepped between the containers, and swung his rifle from his shoulder to a ready position.

The stretch of the east fence on the other side of the containers had collapsed, similar to the south fence where they had entered. Ten yards past the eastern fencing, on the grass between the forest and the container yard, the German shepherd lay bleeding out into the soil, bitten to death, two large Doberman pinschers standing over it, heaving with sharpening growls, their teeth bared in Cole's direction, saliva dancing from their muzzles.

"Bruce! Shit!" Cole kept his rifle ready, stock to shoulder, iron sights hovering near his cheekbone. He took a step backward.

Then, his eyes shifted focus, past the dogs, to the tree line, where he saw the figure of a woman standing between two trees. She was pale, late forties with forgiving eyes, desperation in her features, wearing a white long-sleeve shirt and jeans.

He turned away, felt the metal of a container at his back, leaned against it. "My rifle is me," he said, low, audible only in his mind. "I am my rifle."

He inhaled and exhaled slow and long.

Then, *"Sheryl!"* he yelled. *"Run! Bruce is dead! Run!"*

He turned and ducked out of the channel between containers, into the long aisle of the container yard, heading back the way he'd come, moving in a tactical stance, his gun-side foot slightly behind the other, knees slightly bent, steady, quick steps, rifle up and oscillating. The two men that had been mid-aisle were closer now, not expecting Cole's sudden reappearance. With a quick wave of his rifle and two twitches of his trigger finger, two loud cracks reverberating through the morning, two flashes of fire at the end of his barrel, both men dropped, each with a bullet in the brain. Cole shifted his aim toward the cluster of tents to his right, squeezing off two more shots, dropping two more pirates, one falling back into a tent's canvas, collapsing it.

Return fire began, as he expected, loud pops crackling from the west side of the aisle, the whistle of bullets surrounding him. He dropped to his right knee, directed the rifle up toward the top of a container to his right, targeted a bulky man wearing a full grenade vest and firing down with a submachine gun, another pirate on the opposite end of the container shooting haltingly with a bolt-action rifle, a campfire between them. A bullet from Cole's SCAR-H slammed into the shoulder of the man with the vest, spinning him 90 degrees, dropping him into the fire. He lay stunned for less than a second, then screamed and scrambled to escape the flames without falling from the container. Cole, moving again, had already killed three more pirates along the tops of other containers when the man's vest exploded, killing him and the other pirate on the same container, sending timber and fire and their torsos skyward.

Cole felt a blistering sear on the fringe of his left shoulder, though no jolting force of impact—he knew it was a graze, albeit a deep one.

One of the pirates, a woman, sprang out from behind one of the containers along the east fence to Cole's left with a shotgun, though distance and poor marksmanship kept Cole clear from the spread. Surprised, he dove, turning his shoulder down into a body roll to his right, came up firing two shots, and the woman fell.

Cole lifted himself into a run, firing at movements along the tops of the containers, dipping his rifle to the shadows along the bases of them. A hot fire stabbed through his left shoulder around his collar bone. He fell back with the impact of the bullet, let his lower momentum carry him into a slide forward across the earth, his rifle clicking empty as he rose back to his knees. He clutched the spare ammo clip that was taped upside-down to the side of the clip currently loaded, turned it over, and slapped it into his rifle, a reload in less than two seconds. He kicked himself back to a standing position, aimed at a pirate running out to block his path to the downed south fencing, and managed to hit him in the top left of the head with a calculated spray of bullets before he felt his right kneecap torn away by lead. Cole fell back to his knees, but kept shooting. He held the trigger down through a lateral swing, and three shadows fell, dead or injured. A bullet punched through Cole's gut, another his left ankle, obliterating muscle and tendon. He wrangled himself into position and balanced the iron sights to his eye for a shot that took out the neck of man running at him with an axe.

Epicenters of heat erupted all over Cole's body, rippling through it, blood flooding over his skin.

Then, he didn't feel any more of the shots that shredded him. His vision was above his flesh now, looking down.

A bullet entered the back right side of his skull. He felt the electricity fleeing his synapses, disintegrating—the last spark, a kind face forgiving him.

Outside of the container yard, on the grass between the fallen stretch of the east fence and the forest, there were no dogs, and there was no woman standing among the trees.

Part Three

Theo

Underneath the dense fiber of the rope-secured cloth, the many hours of stark darkness had robbed Theo Scala of his spacial and chronological orientation. The only readable stimuli were the vibrations and kicks from the road under the tires of the white van, and the shoulder-to-shoulder contact of the sobbing captive next to him. He would have moved for more space if he hadn't been handcuffed in place, his lower back threatening to cramp, a numbness prickling through his legs.

He leaned his head lower, to the left, toward the other captive. "It's okay," he said, not convincing even to himself. "Just please stop."

"There's only two of us now," the other captive said. Theo recognized the voice. It was one of the younger captives—early twenties.

"Two of us in this van," Theo clarified. "They have four vans. We're okay. We're okay, okay?"

"Yeah, but what does it matter? The numbers, they keep…"

"These fuckers pick up new ones all the time."

"New ones? So, what, we're supposed to rely on that? On the percentages staying the same? 'Cause sooner or later everyone's chamber is going to be filled."

Theo shook his covered head. "Okay, well, fuck it then. I was just trying to make you feel better—get you to quit the fucking crying for a second. I can't take it anymore."

"Yeah? Fuck you, I'm sorry, okay? I'm just… I'm fucking losing it. I mean, the fucking games they make us play. I remember you from the last one. What the fuck is that? They're fucking savages!"

"Yeah they are."

"So how the fuck could I not be losing it right now? You saw that shit! The poor guy's head opened up like a watermelon. Like a fucking… melon."

"He lost the game."

"What?"

"He lost the game. Poor dumb fucking bastard. He lost the game! I'm glad it wasn't me. Right? We have to make sure it isn't us. That's all we can do."

"Yeah, but there're two of us."

"There's more."

"In the other vans?"

"Yeah."

"Yeah, I'm not so sure. And since that incident? They must have lost over half their numbers. There's only so many of us they can afford to drag along anymore. They may even have had to leave a van or two behind."

"Well—" Theo stopped talking as he felt the van slowing, the pull of a left turn's gravity. The van remained at low speed. "We've slowed down. Please, let us be stopping—I've had to go the bathroom for hours."

"Just go, man. It's okay. I went hours ago," the other captive said.

"I know you did," Theo said. "I can still smell it."

"You know," the younger man started. "I don't think I can take—"

The van settled to a stop, the engine rattling into silence.

Theo heard the murmur of distant voices outside the van, heard a rummaging from the enclosed front cabin of the van, the driver's door slam. After a few seconds, the voice of the pirates' leader, recognizable by its loud gravely bark, was audible: "Get them out of the van!"

"Which one, Silas?" another man's voice said.

"Which one?" Silas said. "The one you were just fucking driving, shit-bird."

The rear doors of the van clicked, squeaked, then thudded open, a slight light leaking up from the small seam between materials at Theo's chest, an abrupt wave of freezing air filling his awareness. He shuddered immediately, involuntarily. His handcuffs jerked, snapped free of his wrists, and a burly hand grabbed his right arm, squeezed hard, pulled him toward the open doors. He went with the pull, ducking his head, thankful there was still enough blood in his legs for balance before dropping from the van. With no ability to gauge the distance to the ground, Theo let momentum carry him to his knees after his boots crunched into snow-covered earth. The cold of the soft ice cut through the legs of his jeans.

He heard the other captive drop next to him.

A white brightness cauterized his vision as the hood was pulled from his head. He clamped his eyelids shut, turned his head away and to the left out of instinct, though the brightness was everywhere. White strobed through his mind. His senses began to adjust, and he cracked his eyes to a squint.

"Welcome to Wyoming, boys!" Silas said loudly.

Wide, flat, snow-caked land sharpened into focus, starred with constellations of jagged, blackened tree trunks—victims of a massive forest fire—stretching fully to the low horizon, the sky big and hazy with steam and frost in the sunlight.

Theo looked to his right, at the other captive, lying face down in the snow, hood still covering his head, maybe unconscious, maybe feigning death. Silas, tall and broad—6'7" with biceps that stretched the sleeves of his leather jacket—did not wait for the captive to show life.

"So," he said, throwing a large wool blanket, a cross-patterned dark blue and gold, between the two captives, "there's only one blanket, and two of you. You know what that means, don't you?"

The other captive was still face down, unmoving.

"Wake that son-of-a-bitch up, Leonard," Silas said, and the

driver of the van they had been riding in stepped forward and kicked the limp captive sharply, eliciting still no reaction.

Theo saw a grouping of three motorcycles to his left and two other white vans to his right, five pirates migrating from the vehicles to the developing scene. One of the pirates was roughly escorting four captives—three women and a man—from the other vans.

"Okay." Silas pulled a .50 caliber Desert Eagle handgun from a holster at his waist, drew back the hammer with his thumb, and pointed it at the captive's head. "He doesn't move, he gets the—"

The captive bucked wildly, shuffled himself quickly to his knees. "Okay, okay!" he said.

"Well, look here. It's a miracle! He's alive after all." Silas pulled the hood from the captive's head, watching him flinch and blink rapidly in the sudden brightness. The pirate pressed the end of the gun's barrel hard into the captive's cheek. "Somehow, I thought he might be." After a terrifying two-second beat, he pulled the gun away. "Now, as I was saying. One blanket, two bastards. That means, for the next ten minutes, my name is Simon."

Shit, Theo thought. The other captive let escape an audible cry.

"And stupid is not doing as Simon says," said Silas. "Alright, alright, both you stand up now. Come on, stand up. Look on the bright side. One of you is about to become the owner of the warmest blanket this side of Wyoming." He chuckled, paced a horizontal four-foot arc in front of them. Theo and the other man stood. "Now, Simon says, as a warm-up, do jumping jacks."

Theo listened to the words carefully, began doing jumping jacks—the alternating pattern of arms and legs spread and together as each jump landed.

"Push-ups now," Silas said.

Neither Theo nor the other captive stopped doing jumping jacks.

"Ha! Good!" The pirate leader twirled his hand in the air as if accepting applause. "Simon says, do push-ups."

Theo's heart dialed faster. He dropped to his knees, and began performing slow, shaky push-ups. He had learned that the pirates didn't really seem to care if he kept his knees on the ground. Even with this form, the exhaustion was excruciating. With how little the pirates fed the captives—sometimes not even human food: dog biscuits and cat chow—Theo was nearing collapse on the fifth push-up. Halfway up on the sixth, his arms wobbling uncontrollably, hands turning numb from the cold, he lost his upward momentum, and began sinking back into the snow.

"Okay, that's enough. Simon says, stand back up," Silas said.

Theo let himself fall to his chest, heaving into the earth, then willed his body slowly to a standing position. Water dripped from the snow in his beard. He felt a wetness begin to seep through the front of his sweater. The other captive stood up next to him.

The pirate captain stepped forward, leaned toward Theo. "You think you're going to win this, don't you?"

Theo looked into Silas's eyes, said nothing.

"You don't just think—you *know* it don't you? After all, you've been with us the longest." Silas leaned in slightly closer. "Don't think I haven't noticed." He chuckled again, backed away. "Alright, alright. Back to it. Simon says… bark like a dog."

Theo had no problem with this humiliation. As degrading as it was, it required low effort, little movement, and minimal depletion of precious energy. He howled into the whitening blue sky. He barked loudly and steadfastly.

To the other captive, the task took far more of a mental toll, which Theo knew was the pirates' main aim. Tears deluged the young man's face as he barked between giant cries, loud sobs he leaned into like taking refuge in a reservoir. Theo could tell that the man was broken—as broken as so many of the captives he had seen before.

He looked away from the young man, past the pirates that now stood watching in a circle around them, to the remaining captives, standing and shivering with their hands cuffed behind their backs. One of the three women had her head down, glancing up at the scene at occasional intervals; another never looked up from the snow at the toes of her shoes. The third woman kept her chin level to the earth, observing the game with a steady resolve. Theo didn't recognize the male captive—late fifties or early sixties with an emptiness in his eyes—whose face was also up, watching. He was new—must have been picked up within the past week. *Poor bastard*, Theo thought, *might not even realize he's next.*

"Stop," Silas said.

Both captives kept barking.

Silas torqued his neck, leaned fast and abruptly toward the captive next to Theo.

"I said, fucking stop!" he yelled, his voice like an amalgam of imagined injury from the mouth of every shadowed alley Theo had ever crossed in his life in New York City before the chaos—before what he labeled in his mind, *The Hellscape.*

The other captive flinched acutely, and stopped barking.

"Uh oh! Whoops!" Silas said, his tone mocking. "Simon didn't say!"

The captive looked throat-punched, blank—then he recoiled, turning sharply to the left, away from the gun, hunching down, raising his right fist to shield his cranium in an instinctive, protective gesture. Silas raised the silver-plated barrel, adjusting to his victim's movement, firing down, the large-caliber bullet plowing through the back of the captive's hand, the back right of his skull, taking apart the majority of his head into the snow. The bang of the gunshot belted through Theo's chest and shoulders, descending his spine.

Everything seemed close—the pirate, the captive's dead body, the pistol-barrel smoke ascending between them. Silas leaned in toward Theo, the pores on his face between his eyes and beard landing into focus, the smell of spent gunpowder spiking Theo's nostrils.

"You owe me one," he said, his pale blue eyes firing with a routine intensity, like a switchblade held constantly outward. He turned and walked toward the remaining captives, stopped and quarter-turned back to Theo.

"Well," he said. "Go ahead. The blanket's yours. Pick up your prize."

Theo, against his stupor, fervently grabbed the blanket from the snow and flagged it out onto his own shoulders. He shivered into its wool.

Silas had already turned back to the other captives.

"Okay, you and you—" He pointed at two of the women, one of them the owner of the resolute face Theo had observed earlier. "Despite all the snow that's about to pour, I declare a thumb war!"

Tera

When Tera pinned the other woman's wriggling right thumb beneath her own, she immediately saw the desperate panic that flooded her eyes. The *I will do fucking anything* panic. Tera and the woman turned in circles in the snow, their right arms bending and twisting and locked at the hands. Tera felt the force of the woman's thumb, wiggling and worming under her grip.

"Two!" The pirate captain—whom another pirate had called Silas—was two-thirds through his count.

Feeling the woman's thumb slipping, Tera gambled. She released the woman's thumb, rotated their clenched fists counterclockwise, twisting, dropping her right elbow down and inward, then re-gripping with her thumb, planting it hard. The strategy worked—the woman's desperately searching thumb entrapped again, more securely.

"Oh, that's a recount! Gotta start it over!" Silas said, pandering to the small surrounding crowd of pirates and captives.

Tera squeezed the woman's thumb hard, her lips parting, her top teeth digging into their bottom counterparts.

"One!" Silas began again.

The flat white-coated land, pocked by the thousands of burned and broken trees spearheading from its soil, seemed to spin around them—this group, these two captured women.

"Two!" Silas shouted.

The other captive woman screamed, wound her left leg, and drove it into Tera's right kneecap.

At this juncture of the game, Tera expected foul play. She had been through enough of these games to know that the other captives were capable of anything when pushed toward death's certainty. She had been trying to keep herself in a versatile stance, and when the kick came, she slid her right leg backward, though the angle of the attack was impossible to escape entirely. The woman's left heel struck the top of her kneecap with enough velocity to push it backward, into itself and further, hyperextending the joint.

Pain fired from the sprain, partially torn ligaments, and Tera yelled, but held the other woman's thumb, and replanted her right foot into the snow.

Then the woman's hand came down, a flash of shadow across the sky's light, without Tera realizing it had been raised, and its long, cracked and jagged nails raked across her face, her right eye closing just in time to avoid being blinded.

Tera felt blood on her face, opened her eyes to see it falling into the snow, realized she was now on her knees, no longer holding the woman's hand, no longer battling in the game.

The other woman, breathing in heaves, thrust a bluing fist toward the sky's white, a grunting cry grating from her throat.

"Enough!" Silas shouted. "The game's decided." The large pirate stepped forward and looked down at Tera. "Tsk-tsk. Such a shame," he pointed the cartoonishly large pistol down at her, "to have a game ruined by rule-breaking." His aimed changed in an instant, the barrel rising to aim square into the other woman's face, which seemed to come apart as he pulled the trigger, a smattering of brain and skull across Tera's perspective of the sky from her back against the snowy earth. She heard fragments and droplets hit the snow around her.

Silas's giant hand appeared a foot above her. She reached out and was yanked to her feet.

He stood close, at least a foot taller than her, looking down, her smaller hand clenched in his thick winter glove, his breath visible through his heavy beard.

"Well done," he said. "Winner, winner. The sleeping bag is yours." He looked over at one of the other pirates. "Hey, dumb-fuck, give her the fucking sleeping bag."

The pirate, a skinny, slightly hunched man with more teeth missing than not, nodded manically and kicked the bound orange sleeping bag toward Tera. The bundle rolled to her feet, and she quickly wrestled its strings untied, whisked down the zipper, and cocooned herself within it, a flap hugging each shoulder. Her breathing slowed under its relief. She stepped backward until she stood next to the black-haired man who had won the blanket in the previous game.

"Alright, final game!" Silas shouted, marching toward the final two captives—an early-sixties-ish man and a mid-twenties woman. He tossed a smooth baseball-sized stone up and down lightly in his hand. With his other hand, he pointed from one captive to the other.

Tera watched the older man's expression worsen.

Silas continued, "Hot potato, hot potato, hot—" He stopped. His posture straightened, his eyes searching the older captive. "What the fuck is that?"

The captive looked down at his own chest. Part of a gold chain hung from under the collar of his jacket in a short glinting loop. His fingers fumbled with it before he managed to stuff it back down under his clothes.

"No, no, no. Let's see it," Silas said. "What was that?"

The captive hesitated, looked shaken, devastated. "It's nothing," he said, his voice rough. "A worthless fake gold chain."

"Let's have it. Bring it back out."

"It's worthless. Only sentimental."

"Bring it back out!"

The captive flinched at the shout, closed his eyes and tilted his head slightly away. He reached beneath his collar and brought the necklace fully out to rest on top of his clothes, against his chest. A gold heart-shaped locket hung from the chain, the sunlight making it gleam as the man breathed.

"Ah, that doesn't look so worthless to me," Silas said.

"I promise you—" the captive started.

"In fact, that looks pretty sparkly. And we like sparkly things." Silas looked over his shoulder at one of the female pirates, who looked back at him. "We like sparkly things, don't we, Sharla?"

The female pirate smiled and nodded, the spaces between her teeth filled with black. "We sure do, Silas."

Silas turned back to the male captive. "You hear that? See? We like sparkly things just fine." He held out his hand. "So go ahead and hand it over."

The captive let out a heavy breath, visible in the cold. "No," he said.

From Tera's angle, she couldn't see Silas's expression, but she could picture it. She had never seen or heard a captive refuse a pirate's demands.

There was a brief silence, and Silas laughed. He raised the gun. "Bold motherfucker, aren't you?" He drew back the gun's hammer with his thumb, a solid metallic clack. "I ain't going to ask you again, compadre."

The captive hesitated, then reached with both hands to the back of his neck and unfastened the necklace. He held it up, but not out, almost as if it was for himself, his eyes watching the heart sway in the air. He re-gripped it, turning it and letting it fold into the palm of his other hand, and clenched it with all five fingers.

"No," he said again. "Sorry, but—"

The Desert Eagle boomed twice and Tera's shoulders lurched. Her eyes were fixed on the captive's face, but saw his chest explode red against the backdrop of snow and light as the man fell back onto the white earth.

Silas walked over to the body in the following silence, his boots audibly biting into the snow. The hulking man lowered himself and pried the dead man's fingers from the locket and chain. He straightened with the locket between his pointer fingers and thumbs, turned it over.

"Who the fuck is Bryce?" Silas said, then turned the locket back around and clicked it open. His shoulders dipped, and for a full two seconds his face lost its character. "Fuck." He clicked the locket shut.

Silas turned to the pirate named Sharla.

"Here you go," he said, and tossed it at her.

Nora

Nora stared at the stranger's dead body, still convinced she knew him. Not just by his face, but his eyes. She had seen them before. During a moment she couldn't place, but was imbued with a mutual trauma.

The man's blood darkened and melted the snow around him.

An array of sentiment pulled at Nora: pity and sadness, gratitude that she didn't have to face him in the pirate's proposed game, revulsion from the gore, and the gravity of familiarity that she tried to brush aside—guilt that inexplicably overwhelmed her emotions more than her brain could reason.

Her knees hit the snow next to the expanding red. Her body hummed in the Wyoming cold.

Nora had never thought she would witness such death in her life—by sheer numbers or cruelty—her husband and her parents among all the others—a long spill of blood—and yet somehow she had become acclimated to her condition, as if a callous had formed thick around her heart.

Her eyes lifted to see the pirates' leader, Silas, sling the locket he had taken from the man's body at a female pirate, who grabbed at it clumsily, dropped it and picked it up.

Silas turned and walked rapidly over to the two winners of the previous games, a man and a woman, standing in close proximity to the one white van parked separate from the other two. The large pirate raised the gun to the male captive's face.

"Looks like you have to play again, buck-o!" he said. "Let's go."

The man's already pale skin whitened beneath his shoulder-length jet-black hair. He pulled the blanket tighter against his shoulders.

"C'mon," he said. "I just played."

"Yeah, well, we need a player." Silas motioned with his head. "Numbers just got uneven."

"You got your loser. Over there."

"He didn't play the game. I'm not going to ask—"

"Silas?" one of the other pirates said, stepping toward his leader. He was a short, filthy man with boils on his face. He had been standing next to the pirate named Leonard. "Look." He pointed to Silas's left, his voice wary and confused.

Silas turned. "The fuck is that?"

Nora followed his eyes. In the opposite direction of the sun, the horizon seemed to disintegrate into the white, tree trunks swallowed by a massive white wall barreling toward the small group of pirates and their captives.

Silas's jaw slackened. "Fuck that, it's a fucking whiteout!" He looked at the pirate who had just spoken. "When was the last time you checked the radio?"

The shorter pirate looked defensive. "Yesterday, but I—"

Silas raised the Desert Eagle and fired a shot into the man's chest.

"Fucking moron!" he said. "Get in the vans!"

The pirates around Nora began running toward the two vans parked together. Nora watched them go, then turned back, saw the male captive lunge at Silas, throwing the wool blanket over his head like a net. He slammed both his palms into Silas's shoulders, simultaneously tucking his foot behind Silas's right calf. Surprised and off balance, Silas fell backward onto the splintered remnants of a tree trunk, the fire-hardened wood knifing through him—into his lower back and out from his stomach—impaling him like a harpoon. As he landed, his arm swung up, and he managed to snap off a wild shot with the pistol, clipping the male captive in the top left of the head, enough for the large caliber to shatter skull, flinging a wide lasso of blood through the air. The captive's body dropped heavily onto the snow.

"Fuck!" Silas yelled. His mouth was already bubbling red. He was alone now—the other female captive and Leonard had already scrambled into the closest van—the captive through the backdoors and Leonard diving into the front cabin.

Nora looked at the blizzard. It was less than a hundred yards away now, and closing in quickly. She looked toward the other two vans. The pirates had reached them, were now inside.

She turned back to Silas and sprinted at him.

As she approached she saw that the giant pistol had fallen from his grip, and now laid beneath its own imprint in the snow. Her feet slushed to a stop. Her eyes oscillated over the feet in front of her—the blanket, the gun's location, the heaves of Silas's chest steadily slowing, becoming heavier, more desperate and fluid-filled, his head already dropped back and bobbing limply.

With match-strike movement, Nora grabbed up the blanket, the heavy pistol, folded the pistol into the blanket, and bunched it all into her arms.

She turned toward the lone van just as the white wall struck.

The blizzard hit like fire on the skin, knocked her sideways as she reached for the van's rear door handle, her left hand still squeezing the blanket against her torso. She fell, her right hip dipping and rolling in dense snow. The freezing thrust of the twisting air scalded her face, her eyes watering shut, immediately hedged with frost. She pulled her collar up over her face, stood, rubbed her shirt into her eyes with a thumb and forefinger. She reached again for one of the van's rear door handles, nearly blind, and instead felt the faint warmth of another human hand clutch her own, pull her up and forward into the van's rear cabin. She smelled metal, upholstery, and the sour human odor of those in their most desperate condition. She heard one of the rear doors slam shut, the piercing howl of the icy tempest suddenly hushed.

Nora lowered her collar from her face, blinked into the floor of the cabin. She could feel the vibration of the van's engine. She looked to her right, lifted herself onto the bench seat that ran the length of one side of the van, discovered that she was sitting across from the other female captive, wet tangled auburn hair and vibrant green eyes, shoulders crowned by the sleeping bag she had won in the demented game of thumb war.

"Thank you," Nora said.

The woman nodded. "You're welcome. You okay?"

"Yeah, I think so." She wiped thawing frost from around her mouth with the back of her hand. "I'm Nora."

"Tera."

"Out there," Nora motioned with her head, "Silas, their leader. He's dead."

"I saw. How many—"

The van's left rear door swung open, the wind's scream and cold again filling the back cabin, and a thin male figure wearing a ski mask lifted himself into the van, his boots landing heavy between the bench seats. He slammed the door, returning the outside rush to a distant whistling. The van rocked from the force of the blizzard. The man pulled down the bottom of his mask. Nora recognized him—Leonard, the pirate who had been in the van's front seat when she had approached. His eyes were abnormally wide and searching. Acne-scarred skin was barely visible beneath his wispy, straggly beard.

"Hey," he said. "Thought I might get kinda lonely up front."

Nora's stomach twisted into itself.

"No, not like that," he said, looking from one woman's face to the other. He held up his hands in a gesture pleading innocence. "It's just, we might be stuck in this blizzard for a while. It'd be nice to have some company."

Neither woman spoke. He stepped past them and sat down on Nora's side of the van, about an arm's length away from her. He scratched at the wool covering his forehead, sniffed loudly. He looked at both of them again. They sat rigid, unmoving.

"Look, first off, I'm not that bad." he said. "I'm not like them. I've never killed nobody before. I'm just—I just try to survive. Like everyone else."

"Like everyone else?" Nora spoke before she realized she was speaking. Her tone was razored with sarcasm.

Leonard looked at her. "Yes. Like everyone." His hands, resting on his knees, turned upward. "You remember when this all started? You remember the president's last transmission? He said, 'Find your people, and stay with them. Survive.' And I did. I didn't have any people, but I did anyway. I had to."

Nora looked across the van at Tera, who studied him, nodding with unconvinced eyes.

Nora turned back to Leonard. "You found your people, huh? Your people? You watched them kill us."

"Wait a minute," Leonard said.

"You watched us all fucking die. You fucking killed us!" Nora's right hand dug subtly into the blanket in her lap, found the barrel of the enormous pistol, began turning it through the wool.

"Look, I—"

Nora's hand met the handle of the Desert Eagle, and she stripped it free of the blanket's contours. Her left hand came up, its fingers meeting the fingers of her right hand as she gripped, and aimed, and pulled the trigger. The detonation of the shot was magnified in the cabin, a concussive punch of sound, and the gun jackhammered backward, slamming into Nora's face, bringing everything into nothingness.

#

Nora woke dizzy, Tera's voice in her ear and frail cold grasp on her forearm. Nora's face throbbed, felt stiff with the iron crust of drying blood. She spit onto the van's floor—fresh red thickened by dehydration.

"Nora," she heard Tera say. "You okay?"

"Is he—?" Nora started, but didn't finish her question as she looked left into a head with no face, a crater, blood running out onto the seat and the floor, puddling. She looked away, up at Tera, lifted herself back to the bloodless part of the bench. Her hands shook hard.

Tera was leaning forward, hands still outstretched to help, eyes worried.

Nora nodded at her. "I'm okay," she said. After a few shaky breaths, "You okay?"

Tera straightened, blinked. "Yeah, I'm okay."

"Okay." Nora looked around the van. The incessant pain in her face interfered with her thoughts. She placed an index finger from each hand on her temples. "Okay. I'm going for the front seat." She grabbed the blanket, now spattered with blood, from where it had fallen on the seat, and wrapped it around herself.

"But the blizzard."

"I'll make it."

"We don't know how bad it's got."

Nora looked at her. "I'll risk it. I need to know what's going on out there as it happens. I can honk the horn when the blizzard's lightened up enough for you to join me."

"I don't know."

Nora stood and placed a hand on the right door handle. "Stay here. You're going to be alright." She breathed. "Hold on to the gun."

Nora knew the blizzard had worsened as soon as she stepped back out into it, closing the door behind her. Every centimeter of exposed skin seared. The wind knocked her backwards, almost off her feet. She tried to push forward against it, but then collapsed and began crawling through the swirling and thickening ground snow. She turned up the driver's side of the van and pulled herself across the ground, her fingers growing more numb with each hand plant. She vaguely realized she was screaming with the physical exertion, her voice suffocated by the wind's howl. She reached the door to the front cabin, found its handle, and pulled herself up by it. She paused, timing the moment, then used all her strength and body weight to yank open the door against the wind, between its heavier gusts, and forced herself inside. The wind slammed the door after her.

Nora waited in the driver's seat, her head down and hands on the wheel, for her breathing to slow. She tilted her head, seeing the keys in the ignition. She pulled down the sun visor, looked into its mirror. Her face was bright red from windburn. There was a gash across the bridge of her nose, which looked broken, both her eyes bloodshot and ringed by purple. Another larger gash ran between her eyebrows. Her cheeks were emaciated from malnutrition, her cheekbones more defined and jutting. She closed the visor and turned up the van's heating, holding her hands out over the vents. Nothing but white was visible outside the windows. She closed her eyes.

She considered how all of this happened, how she found herself here, in this seat in this van in this world, and it occurred to her that this whole thing, the destruction across the planet, the deaths of her family, her imprisonment and torture, all of it, happened for her to learn this truth right now, this second, about what she was capable of.

She opened her eyes, and reached for the radio dial.

Jacob Minasian received his MFA from Saint Mary's College of California, where he was the 2016 Academy of American Poets prize-winner. He is the author of the full-length poetry collection *Vestiges* (2023), and the chapbook *American Lit* (2020), and his work has appeared in publications including, among others, *Poets.org, The Museum of Americana, RipRap Literary Journal, Lucky Jefferson, Windows Facing Windows Review, CP Quarterly, Red Ogre Review,* multiple anthologies, and has been nominated for a Pushcart Prize. Originally from California, he currently lives with his wife and daughter in Cincinnati, Ohio.

www.ingramcontent.com/pod-product-compliance
Lightning Source LLC
Chambersburg PA
CBHW020238030726
47497CB00009B/3148